From Megan Maitland's Diary

Dear Diary,

Things are getting out of hand with all this ridiculous publicity, and I hate feeling so helpless. R.J. gets more withdrawn each day, but oh, Dana puts him on his ear! She's just what he needs, though I doubt he's realized it yet. I want to spend more time with him, but there's so much going on, so much that has to be tended to—what with the reporters here constantly, and that witch Tanya Lane stirring up trouble. And now—I can scarcely believe it!—Connor is back!

And the baby. I do so love that baby. I suppose I'll just have to trust Dana to see to R.J.'s needs. Heaven knows she's been doing so for years. In many ways, she's as close to R.J. as

his family. I love her.

I wonder when R.J. will wake up to the fact that he loves her, too.

Dear Reader,

There's never a dull moment at Maitland Maternity! This unique and now world-renowned clinic was founded twenty-five years ago by Megan Maitland, widow of William Maitland, of the prominent Austin, Texas, Maitlands. Megan is also matriarch of an impressive family of seven children, many of whom are active participants in the everyday miracles that bring children into the world.

As our series begins, the family is stunned by the unexpected arrival of an unidentified baby at the clinic— unidentified, except for the claim that the child is a Maitland. Who are the parents of this child? Is the claim legitimate? Will the media's tenacious grip on this news damage the clinic's reputation? Suddenly, rumors and counterclaims abound. Women claiming to be the child's mother materialize out of the woodwork! How will Megan get at the truth? And how will the media circus affect the lives and loves of the Maitland children—Abby, the head of gynecology, Ellie, the hospital administrator, her twin sister, Beth, who runs the day care center, Mitchell, the fertility specialist, R.J., the vice-president of operations— even Anna, who has nothing to do with the clinic, and Jake, the black sheep of the family?

Please join us as the mystery of the Maitland baby unravels, bit by enticing bit, and book by captivating book!

Marsha Zinberg,
Executive Editor

LORI FOSTER

Married to the Boss

Silhouette Books

Published by Silhouette Books

America's Publisher of Contemporary Romance

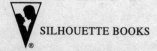 SILHOUETTE BOOKS

ISBN-13: 978-0-373-65064-4

Recycling programs
for this product may
not exist in your area.

MARRIED TO THE BOSS

Copyright © 2000 by Harlequin Books S.A.

Lori Foster is acknowledged as the author of this work.

Visit Silhouette Books at www.eHarlequin.com

Printed in U.S.A.

Lori Foster's first book, first book, a Harlequin Temptation, was published in January 1996. Her second book launched the BLAZE subseries. Since then, she's seen more than sixty of her books make their way into print, has written several novellas and has published with a variety of different houses.

Lori has been a recipient of the prestigious *RT Book Reviews* Career Achievement Award for Series Romantic Fantasy, and for Contemporary Romance. She's had top-selling books for Amazon, Waldenbooks and the BGI Group. For more about Lori, visit her website at www.lorifoster.com.

To Emily Toerner,
A gem for a gem. I couldn't have chosen better myself,
and that surely puts my mother's heart at ease.

CHAPTER ONE

As soon as R. J. Maitland turned into the sweeping drive of Maitland Maternity Clinic, he saw the mob. Not a rioting mob, but every bit as bloodthirsty. *Reporters*.

They wouldn't destroy property, but they were certainly doing their best to destroy his reputation and that of the clinic. As president of Maitland Maternity, he felt responsible for its good name.

As a man, he felt a red-hot rage.

His hands tightened painfully on the wheel of his Mercedes, the only sign he allowed of his inner turmoil. Damn Tanya Lane for naming him as the father of the abandoned baby. And damn himself for having ever been involved with her in the first place.

Hoping to go unnoticed by the milling, impatient crowd, he drove to the parking lot around the corner. It turned out to be a futile effort; his car was spotted, and the mob rushed his way, flashbulbs popping, video cams zooming in, reporters with microphones extended, running to reach him, hoping for the first damaging quote of the day.

Since the baby had been discovered on the steps of

the clinic in September, it had been like this, but now the focus had changed. He was the target.

Though his anger was near the boiling point, he remained outwardly aloof, ignoring them all and walking with an unhurried stride to the door. A security guard stood there, ready to block out the unwelcome press, but it wasn't easy getting past them. Questions were shouted at him, questions he couldn't honestly answer, and that made the rage all the worse.

"R.J.! Are you the father of the baby?"

"What do you intend to do about your child?"

"How does your family feel about this unexpected turn of events?"

He'd been asking himself the same things over and over again, ever since the basket with the little boy had been left at the clinic with a note claiming that he was a Maitland. Now, of course, the situation was worse.

Tanya Lane, an ex-girlfriend, had deliberately labeled him the father.

He forged onward, his jaw locked, his hands curled into fists. Just as he stepped through the polished brass-and-glass door, another reporter shouted loudly, "R.J., do you think you and Ms. Lane will reconcile now?"

R.J. stopped in midstep, then turned with fatal deliberation, jaw set, eyes hard. He sought out the reporter, who blinked owlishly in response to his visible fury, and with icy disdain said, "No."

A hush settled over the reporters with the finality of that single word, then they quickly erupted with more questions. Damn it, he knew better than to respond to the press at all. It was best to simply ignore them, to claim *no comment.* But he was sick and tired of their barbs, and he was fed up with being labeled as the type of bastard who would walk away from his responsibilities. He was used to controlling his life, to adjusting events, plans and people to suit his purposes. But in this, he had little control at all. It was intolerable.

Turning his back on the throng of reporters, R.J. headed into the clinic while the doorman struggled to close the door behind him. *Reconcile with Tanya?* he thought with acid disgust. *Not in this or any other lifetime.* He hadn't seen the woman for months. If it hadn't been for that TV reporter Chelsea Markum, offering a paltry bribe to get the negligent mother to come forth, he probably still wouldn't have heard from Tanya. Their parting hadn't been particularly pleasant, but it had been final.

At the time, Tanya had accepted his decision, taking the farewell money he offered her and walking away— as he'd known she would. She'd said nothing about a baby, not even about the possibility of a baby. Yet a baby had been left, alone and unprotected, on the clinic doorstep, and that sickened him as nothing else could.

If Tanya Lane was the mother, R.J. thought viciously, she would be wise to stay the hell out of his sight, and well out of his reach.

The elevator was thankfully empty as he rode to the second floor, where his office was located, giving him the few necessary moments to rein in his temper. He wanted, needed to shut himself inside and concentrate on work, on getting back on track. He hoped to find the usual relief in his daily routine, but he doubted he would, given his dark mood.

The second he stepped through the office door he saw Dana Dillinger, his longtime secretary, preparing a cup of coffee. Dana was quietly efficient, totally competent and a balm to his escalating frustration. Somehow, Dana always seemed to know exactly when he would walk in, and she continually found ways to make his work environment as comfortable for him as possible. Today he appreciated that more than ever before.

He eyed her prim back for a moment, watching her economical, graceful movements. "Good morning, Dana."

She looked up at him with a commiserating smile as she stirred just the right amount of creamer into his coffee. As usual, her dark blond hair was neatly swept into a sophisticated twist at the back of her head, and her light gray suit was tailored, perfectly pressed and eminently suitable for the secretary to the president. "I guess you saw the reporters outside?"

"They'd be damn hard to miss."

She didn't so much as flinch at his sarcastic statement. Instead, she followed him into his office with the coffee in one hand and a bagel in the other. "You probably haven't eaten today, have you?"

As well as being a top-notch secretary, Dana had the

tendency to coddle. She was, in fact, the only woman he let get away with it. "I'm fine," he said as he sat in the black leather chair behind his desk.

"No, you're not." Never one to be affected by his moods or surly temper, she set the steaming coffee at his elbow then insistently pushed the bagel in front of him. "Eat. You'll feel better."

He stared at her in disbelief. Feel better? Is that what she thought, that he merely needed to *feel better?* Everything he'd carefully constructed—his reputation, his standing in the community, his contacts and associations—was threatened by the recent scandal. And the reputation of the clinic was undergoing critical speculation.

"Dana," he growled, not bothering to regulate his tone now that he was away from the press, "I seriously doubt a goddamned bagel is going to do much to repair the damage from all the vicious gossip."

She bit her lip, then sighed. As usual, she took his moods in stride, never backing off, never flashing her own temper in return. That, too, was a blessing, allowing him the total freedom to be himself, without having to concern himself about the impression he might give.

At moments like this, she positively amazed him.

"R.J., anyone who knows you realizes you'd never abandon a woman just because she got pregnant. You're far too conscientious for that. Miss Lane's ridiculous story that you got her pregnant and then refused to marry her is just that—utterly ridiculous."

Her overwhelming belief in him made his stomach muscles tighten in response. He watched her, his expression deliberately impassive. "She was no more than a casual, ill-advised fling, Dana. Available for what I wanted, which sure as hell wasn't marriage. I'd hardly rush to the altar with her, regardless of the situation."

Though a blush brightened her fair complexion and her eyes wouldn't quite meet his, she muttered stubbornly, "Maybe not, but you wouldn't abandon her, either. You wouldn't leave her to take care of the situation on her own."

He gave her a hard look, judging her earnestness, then shook his head. In a low, nearly imperceptible whisper, he muttered, "You sound pretty sure of that."

Her chin lifted resolutely. "I am."

R.J. wasn't given to self-doubt or worry, but then, this was a unique situation. No woman had ever dared to try manipulating him as Tanya had, and never before had his honor been questioned. He found himself moving the bagel from one side of the plate to another as he considered his very limited options. A sleepless night had done little to help resolve the issues. He wanted—needed—to talk, to sort out his thoughts, and right now his family had more than enough to deal with. That left Dana as his only sounding board.

Without an ounce of apology, he met her steady gaze and admitted, "It's possible that I could be the father."

Dana stared at him, her expression blank. He'd noticed her wide green eyes before, of course, since they were a focal point of color against her fair skin. But never before had he seen them look so wary. She stood there before him for a frozen moment in time, then suddenly launched into a flurry of efficiency, straightening books on a shelf, putting away a file. When she spoke, her hands nervously and needlessly tidied the subdued twist in her blond hair.

"That's absurd." She didn't meet his gaze, but rather stared at his tie clip as if fascinated by it. "I seriously doubt Miss Lane is even the baby's mother, so how could you be the father? She just wants the five thousand dollars that TV reporter offered, that's all."

R.J. saw the way her straight shoulders had stiffened inside her suit, how her hands, with their short, unpainted nails, were clenched tightly together, turning her knuckles white. Her distress was plain to see, and for one ridiculous moment he wanted to soothe her. He shook off the aberrant sensation.

"I hope you're right," he said quietly, still watching her. "But I did some calculations last night, and the timing works."

Dana closed her eyes and let out a long, shaky breath.

She looked so distraught, he felt a frisson of uneasiness. He grimly tamped it down. "Dana?"

Shaking her head, she turned away and stalked to the window behind his desk. She wrapped her arms around herself in a strangely defensive gesture that he didn't understand, and when she spoke, her voice emerged as a rasp. "You didn't...didn't use protection with her?"

An instinctive flash of anger took him by surprise. He was far too old, and far too private, to be explaining himself or his actions. No one—family, business associates or friends—dared to take him to task. Under normal circumstances he would have responded to such a question with contempt.

But he supposed he'd invited the query by bringing up the topic. He almost grinned as he considered her question. Never would he have imagined having such a discussion with his professional-to-the-bone secretary. Dana was so straitlaced, so proper, R.J. doubted she understood the most basic aspects of hot, gritty lust. But he certainly did, and he'd long ago learned to utilize his icy self-control even during the most heated moments, refusing to be drawn in by any woman, refusing to take unnecessary chances. His sense of responsibility and his natural inclination to have the upper hand had always kept him safe from any long-term commitments—and fathering a baby would definitely be considered long term.

Though he was half amused, he also resented Dana's lack of faith. "Of course I took precautions," he said coolly, letting her feel his displeasure over her implications. "In this day and age, only an idiot wouldn't, and I promise you, I'm not an idiot."

She looked startled. "I never meant—"

He cut her off, not wanting to hear her clarify her

doubts. "Nothing is foolproof, Dana, you should know that. But if Tanya did get pregnant, this is the first I've heard about it."

The tightening grip of rage he'd been experiencing ever since the baby had been found threatened to break his control.

Damn it, he didn't want his reputation trashed just because he'd made an error in judgment. He should never have slept with Tanya, but he hadn't realized what a conniving bitch she was at the time. She'd claimed to want the same things as he, and that damn sure didn't include being a parent. But if a baby had been conceived, she should have known him well enough to realize he would never disregard his obligations.

R.J. came to his feet, hating the look he'd seen on Dana's face, one of disappointment, when all he'd ever seen there before was admiration and respect. He wouldn't tolerate it. He clasped her shoulders and turned her to face him, aware suddenly of how small she seemed. If she leaned forward, she'd be able to nestle against his chest perfectly.

That errant observation took him by surprise, and he ground his teeth together. He wanted to shake her, more out of anger at himself than at Dana.

"If I am the father, she never bothered to tell me. All that garbage about me refusing to marry her, to acknowledge the baby—it's all lies. I'd *never* turn my back on my responsibilities. You know that, Dana."

His statement demanded that she agree. She looked

at him, her eyes liquid, as if she were on the verge of crying, which didn't make a damn bit of sense. Dana never showed excesses of emotion. She handled his office and his business affairs with a remarkable competence that sometimes left him awed, but she never got emotionally involved. In all the time he'd known her, he'd never seen so much as a hint of her personal side. When she was sick, she stoically denied it. When she was tired, she hid it. If she'd ever been hurt, or if she'd ever grieved, he knew nothing about it. Even though his sister Abby and Dana were longtime friends, Dana's personal life was a mystery to him.

Which was how he'd always wanted it.

As if it had never been there, Dana's tearful expression disappeared. She visibly drew herself together and mustered a shaky smile. R.J. felt as if he'd just taken a punch to the gut. Without meaning to, he tightened his hands on her fragile shoulders.

"I know, R.J.," she said, her gaze unwavering. "You're the most dedicated, reliable, professional person I know. You just… just took me by surprise."

Struck by some unnameable emotion, R.J. released her and stepped back. The urge to pull her closer, to see just how well she might fit against him, had nearly overwhelmed him and he didn't like it. The whole situation was getting out of hand, taking its toll on his lauded control, which he assumed could explain his sudden need for her trust and understanding. But he'd be damned if he let things get to him that much.

With a deceptive calm, he added, "Since she's lied about so many things, I'd be willing to bet Tanya is making every bit of it up. I doubt she's the mother because we have similar acquaintances and someone would have mentioned her being pregnant. And I can't believe I'm the father or she'd have been after me long before now, demanding I pay, if nothing else."

"Which you'd have done."

He gave one sharp nod of agreement. Oh, yeah, he'd have paid, all right, and more. "All I'm saying is that I want to be sure. I want proof."

Dana touched his sleeve. "And until then you can't deny a thing. I understand. Is there anything at all I can do to help?"

R.J. found his first smile of the day. Though Dana was clearly troubled over the possibility that some of the gossip could be warranted, she still managed to be supportive. Outside of his family, she was the one person he'd always been able to count on, and having her trust now lightened his burden. "I should give you a raise, you know."

She smiled, too, looking vaguely smug despite the lingering shadows in her eyes. "You just did two months ago."

"Which obviously proves I'm an intelligent man."

"I won't argue with you there."

She touched him again, just the light press of her fingertips to his wrist, but R.J. felt an unexpected, almost acute pleasure from the small caress. The look on her face went beyond admiration and regard, bordering on something he'd never quite noticed before. He studied her expression before admitting he wasn't sure how to deal with it, or his reaction to that look. He felt an all too familiar tightening in his body—*for Dana?*

"Is there anything I can do to help?" she asked again.

He was still caught up in wondering why she was suddenly affecting him this way. Thinking it through, he decided it could be because his thoughts and emotions had been thrown off base by all the outside turmoil surrounding the scandal. He was likely imagining things where she was concerned, or grasping at any safe line available. And Dana had always been very safe.

Either way, he didn't like it. He stepped away from her with the pretense of getting back to his desk again to eat the bagel. With a casualness he didn't feel, he said, "You've done more than enough, Dana, just by being yourself."

After he said them, it struck him forcefully how true those words were. He twisted to look at her again, trying to decide what it was about Dana that made her so different, so easy to be with.

She wasn't an unattractive woman, he thought, taking note of the soft gray business suit she wore, which made her skin look very pale and luminous, emphasizing the vivid green of her large, almond-shaped eyes.

Her hair, a silky dark blond, was probably long, though he'd never seen it out of its elegant French twist.

He started to wonder further about her hair, trying to imagine it hanging loose, a sleek fall around her breasts. Quickly he drew his thoughts away from that direction and the heated images it conjured. He didn't want to be that curious about her.

Her features were pleasantly balanced, a slim nose, softly rounded cheekbones, a high, smooth forehead. Her ears, which he felt absurd for even noticing, were small and, as usual, adorned with tiny gold studs. Dana wore very little jewelry. In fact, she wore very little adornment of any kind. R.J.'s gaze skimmed her ring-less fingers and her smooth throat, where he realized he'd never seen a necklace. She wore a simple white silk blouse buttoned to the top. There were no clasps in her hair, no bracelets on her delicate wrists, no bows or buckles or frills of any kind on her clothing.

If she wore any makeup, he'd never been able to detect it. But even without mascara, her lashes were slightly darker than her hair, a dusty brown, long and feathery. Her eyes, he decided, bordered on erotic, though he'd never noticed that before. Her lips, without the shine or color of lipstick, were soft and full and damn appealing.

His scrutiny apparently unnerved her. As he watched, her lips parted on a shaky, indrawn breath. His thighs tightened, and his eyes narrowed the tiniest bit in speculation.

When his gaze met hers, she blushed, not a dainty, pretty blush, but an amusing splash of color that made her skin glow and look heated from within. He meant to tease her about what she was thinking, but swallowed the words instead. His own thoughts didn't bear close inspection, and teasing her about what was going on between them could affect their business relationship. That was something he didn't want, even if he was suddenly noticing things about her that he'd never noticed before.

What really drew him, he thought, feeling relief at the sound and reasonable revelation, was her almost eerie sixth sense of what he wanted and needed, and when. She was the perfect secretary, always one step ahead of him, and he intended to keep her solidly in that role.

Dana shifted slightly as the silence dragged on. "R.J.?"

"I'm sorry." He turned back to his bagel and took a healthy bite. "My mind is a little preoccupied today," he said after he'd swallowed.

The tension she'd felt could still be heard in her breathless tone, giving credence to his need for discretion. "No wonder. But it will all work out. You'll see."

"I intend to make sure that it does." He leaned back in his chair, watching her as he finished off the bagel. Silently, he admitted she was right about him being hungry. He'd just been too annoyed to realize it. "I've tried calling Tanya, but either she isn't answering her phone, or she's moved again. I didn't bother to leave a message."

Dana flashed him a look of wry amusement. "Perhaps

since she's fabricated this whole absurd situation, she's decided it's best to avoid any confrontations. Especially with you."

He nodded. "The more people she talks with, the better her chances of mixing up her story."

Dana came hesitantly closer. "Have you considered explaining to the press that this is the first you've heard about Tanya's possible connection to that poor little baby?"

"Mother doesn't think it's a good idea, and since she's the CEO—and basically I agree with her—I'm deferring to her. For the moment, it's best if I keep the lowest profile I can. Tanya will trip herself up soon enough, especially with Chelsea Markum and 'Tattle Today TV' helping her along."

The phone on Dana's desk rang, and she glanced at the outer office with annoyance. "So in the meantime, it's work as usual?"

"I don't see that I have a lot of choice. Besides, I refuse to let those vicious witches or the nosy press totally disrupt our schedule."

She hesitated a moment more, then hurried to the door. "All right," she said on her way out, "but remember, R.J., if you need anything, anything at all, all you have to do is let me know."

The door closed behind her with a quiet click, and R.J. leaned back in his leather chair, thoughtfully considering her words. Given the circumstances, it was a very generous offer. Anyone getting close to him risked being dragged into the limelight, as well.

But to be honest, he'd expected no less of Dana. In the years she'd worked for him, she'd been as loyal and supportive as any person he knew. He could always count on her.

Which was why admitting the truth to her had been so important. He didn't think he was the baby's father, but on the off chance that at least that much of Tanya's story proved to be true, he'd wanted Dana to know about it up front. She deserved as much.

He hated the fact that she might have lost a modicum of respect for him. Having been abandoned himself as a child, and knowing his father to be irresponsible and uncaring, R.J. valued his reputation above all else. He'd always protected it with savage determination.

Seeing his integrity questioned in the press was painful enough. Having Dana doubt him would be unbearable.

CHAPTER TWO

DANA WAS typing up correspondence for the day, getting ahead of herself before R.J. showed up for work in case he needed to talk. She wanted to be there for him in any way she could.

The last few days she'd gladly listened as he'd ranted and railed against the world. The press was having a field day with him, splashing the story across every newspaper in the state. He wasn't sleeping well, she knew, and her heart ached for him. That he needed her now both troubled and appeased her. She hated seeing R.J. in such an untenable situation, knowing how much he valued control. She'd gladly have done anything in her power to make things right for him.

But for the first time that she could recall, he needed her as more than a competent secretary, and her heart swelled with the satisfaction of being the one he turned to.

She'd loved him forever, it seemed.

Not that he knew of her love. Dana had far too much pride to expose her feelings like that. On the rare occasions when R.J. got involved with a woman, if fleeting affairs could be termed as involved, he'd gravitated to the type of sophisticated, sexy femininity that Dana could never achieve. The women he was seen with were elegant and beautiful and confident.

They were everything Dana was not.

R.J. had always treated her with full respect for her abilities in the office, and he was generous to a fault, showing his appreciation for her dedication with raises and hefty holiday bonuses. He gave to her, but never in the way of a personal gift.

Not once had he looked at her as a man looks at a woman he desires. And she knew he never would.

As president of Maitland Maternity and a member of Texas's wealthiest families, R.J. was considered a prime catch. He had money, status and connections—all qualities that drew women in droves.

But Dana knew that even if he'd been dirt poor and unknown in the community, women would have flocked to his side. At thirty-nine, R. J. Maitland was a handsome man in the prime of his life.

He stood easily six feet two inches tall, all of him hard and strong and capable. He had broad shoulders and a lean physique that looked equally gorgeous in a formal tux or well-worn jeans. His hands were large and sure, and he possessed an innate virility that overrode his sophistication, making him seem almost primitive on occasion—just often enough to keep any woman around him slightly breathless and filled with anticipation.

Dana understood that feeling firsthand, because she'd

been close to him for many years now as his personal secretary.

She closed her eyes and sighed, picturing him in her mind. R.J.'s straight sandy hair and probing hazel eyes set him apart from the other Maitlands, who tended toward darker hair and blue eyes.

Dana's love for R.J. meant she'd never even been tempted by another man, though there had been a few times when she'd tried. Dating had been a severe disappointment, and she'd long since decided it was easier to skip it altogether than to suffer the dissatisfaction of being held or kissed by a man she didn't want.

Talking quietly with R.J. about his problems, having him listen to her opinion helped soften the pain of his usual aloofness. Knowing he was upset and that she'd been able to make him smile for just a bit had filled her with conflicting emotions. She felt guilt for enjoying this time with him when he was so obviously burdened with frustration and rage. And she worried because no one could predict how this entire mess would be resolved, or how badly the Maitlands, R.J. in particular, might be hurt in the bargain.

R.J. was a man used to taking charge. In both his work and his personal life, he controlled the people and events around him. But always with a velvet glove, and with the best of intentions. In many ways, he controlled Dana, too, though she fought him on it often, and she knew he respected her for it.

However, in this instance, there was little he could do.

He was virtually helpless against his former girlfriend's spite and the gleeful condemnation of the press, and Dana knew how impossible that would be for R.J. to accept.

She also felt sick with the fear that he might prove to be that little baby's father. She didn't think she could stand it if that happened, but what could she do? She had no claim on him, and reality told her she never would.

Her thoughts were interrupted when R.J. stepped into the office, his face dark with anger after forcing his way through the crowd of reporters who'd been camping outside day after day.

Dana was on her feet in an instant, going to the coffee pot and pouring him his customary cup of sweetened coffee. She shouldn't have let her thoughts get away from her like that. Before she could finish, R.J. growled, "Have you seen the morning paper?"

His tone warned her it wouldn't be pleasant, and she turned warily. "No. I came in early to get some things taken care of. I haven't looked at the paper yet."

R.J. tossed a section of crumpled newspaper on her desk. "There's an entire exposé in there on how wealthy Maitland Maternity president R. J. Maitland has deserted his poor pregnant lover. The suggestion is that I was more than willing to sleep with her, but walked away the second she found out she was expecting. They make me sound like the coldest bastard alive."

The wash of anger took her by surprise. "Those vipers!" Dana set the cup of coffee down with a hard thunk, and some of it sloshed onto the cabinet. She ignored the spill. Snatching up the paper, she quickly read the article, and her temper began to simmer. She felt fiercely protective of R.J., and the unfair way he was being treated was more than she could take. "This is awful—all speculation and innuendo. Pure slander. I think you should sue!"

In an uncharacteristic snit, she viciously wadded the paper into a ball and jammed it into the metal trash can.

R.J.'s brow rose. "I think you may be taking this worse than I did."

Hearing the sudden amusement in his tone, she whirled to face him. "How can you joke right now?" She was nearly strangling with outrage on his behalf, easily imagining how that report had made him feel. "They're saying terrible things about you!"

The minute the words left her mouth, she wished them back. R.J. cared a great deal about his reputation; Dana, who watched him give everything he had to the clinic, knew that better than most. She'd learned long ago that R.J. had been abandoned by his father, Robert, after his mother's death. He and his little sister, Anna, had been adopted and raised by Robert's brother, William, and William's wife, Megan.

William and Megan had loved R.J. as their own son, but R.J. still suffered over the shame of knowing he'd been discarded, left for someone else to raise. He worked hard to prove he was different from his disreputable father, and Dana understood the toll the gossip was taking on him.

Her heart ached, but she knew better than to approach him, to try to hold him. R.J. didn't want that from her. He was satisfied that she be his assistant—so she'd always been the best one possible.

Scrubbing at his face, R.J. turned away. "They're not cutting any corners, I'll grant you that. Every new story gets a little uglier, with a little more speculation thrown in." He muttered a curse just under his breath and shoved his hands into the pockets of his slacks. When he faced Dana again, his eyes were glittering dangerously. "Fifty invitations to the party have been returned with lame excuses."

"You mean people are giving their regrets."

"I mean people are bailing out, plain and simple."

The party, scheduled for March, was to celebrate Maitland Maternity's twenty-fifth anniversary. Five hundred invitations had gone out, and the event was supposed to be a huge success. But now, with invitations being returned… "What are you going to do?"

"I'm not certain yet, though Mother has a few ideas." There was a fleeting smile on his mouth. "She loves that baby, you know."

Dana nodded. Megan Maitland was a friend, and one of the most generous women Dana knew, both with money and with her heart. She had created Maitland Maternity Clinic, with her husband's blessing, out of a need to help all pregnant women, rich or poor. Because of the caring atmosphere Megan cultivated, the clinic in Austin, Texas had quickly become world-renowned.

The family had been announcing the anniversary party to the press the day the baby had been discovered. The timing couldn't have been worse, with so many cameras and reporters already on hand. Megan had shielded the infant as much as she could, and at that moment she'd started to care for him. Dana smiled softly. "I knew when she was given permission to take the baby home as a foster mother, she'd get emotionally involved."

R.J. gave a brief nod. "I think if the note hadn't been there, claiming the baby was a Maitland, she'd still have felt the same." He worked his jaw a moment, then added, "She has in the past."

"Yes." Dana wondered if R.J. was thinking about his own circumstances, or the other children Megan had cared for. But R.J. *was* Megan's son, even if Megan wasn't his birth mother. "She's a very special woman."

"That she is." R.J. tilted his head, and another rare smile touched his hard features. "And speaking of special women…" He withdrew a long velvet box from his inside jacket pocket.

Dana stared at the box. "You bought Megan a gift?"

This time R.J. laughed, startling her with the sound of it. R.J. was rarely given to moods of joviality. A workaholic, he took life seriously and molded it to suit him.

That didn't leave a lot of room for laughter, and lately, there'd been no reason for it at all. "When I said a special woman, I was talking about you, Dana."

"Me?" Her voice squeaked, and she quickly cleared her throat. "What—?"

At her surprise, R.J.'s expression warmed with masculine satisfaction. He stepped closer to her. "Dana, you've always been the perfect secretary, taking care of things before I can even tell you what needs to be taken care of."

"You would expect no less from an employee."

His smile widened. "True. But these last few days you've gone above and beyond the call of duty."

Dana stared at him wide-eyed, her heart thumping heavily in her chest, her legs feeling suddenly weak. He held the box out to her, but she pressed her hands behind her back to avoid touching it. "I don't understand."

She knew she sounded a bit panicked, but she was so afraid to think more of the gesture than what it really meant. She didn't want to do or say anything awkward, anything to make herself look foolish or make R.J. regret—

R.J. reached behind her and caught her hand, drawing it forward. Rather than giving her the box, he enfolded her fingers in his own. Dana felt the incredible heat of his touch, the roughness of his fingertips and palm proving he was more than a desk jockey, that he enjoyed working outdoors and using his hands. He was strong and rugged and thoroughly masculine. She grew warm from the inside out, her skin flushed, her pulse racing with excitement and anticipation.

R.J. moved his big thumb over her knuckles and smiled. "I've been in a black fury all week, thanks to Chelsea Markum. With her promise of a five-thousand-dollar reward, she's practically begging for frauds and trumped-up lies, knowing people will do damn near anything for a lump of cash. I've been made to look like the center attraction in a three-ring circus."

Dana forced aside her own misgivings and nervousness to curl her fingers around his, giving him a reassuring squeeze.

His hazel eyes, glittering with intent, stared into hers. "People who've known me forever are starting to wonder just how accurate the gossip might be."

"That's not true…" she started to say, but R.J. tugged her just the tiniest bit closer, and she swallowed the denial.

"Yes, it is. None of them trust me right now, but you've never wavered."

"Of course not."

His smile this time was self-mocking. "You've made it all bearable, Dana, and I want you to know how much I appreciate that."

She didn't want his appreciation, but what she did want, she couldn't have. "I know you too well to suffer doubts about your character, R.J."

His expression tightened for one timeless moment,

then she felt the velvet box placed in her hand. "I want you to have this."

Thinking she finally understood the gesture, she shook her head. "It's not necessary."

"I know." Some vague emotion flickered in his eyes before his dark lashes dropped to hide the expression. "That's why I got it for you."

With a smile of pure giddy delight, she carefully opened the box, then drew in a startled breath of wonder. Inside, nestled in more velvet, was a dainty, exquisite emerald and diamond pendant. It wasn't ostentatious, but tasteful, the green stone perfectly cut with a border of small shining diamonds, hanging from a delicately woven gold chain.

Dana swallowed, unsure what to say as she stared at the jewelry. She'd never had anything like it. Her mother would have claimed it was wicked, particularly since it had been bought by a man. But then, her mother had hated any type of artificial decoration. She'd taught Dana that proper women didn't indulge in such frivolous advertisement. Her mother thought it looked tacky, and as she'd explained to Dana many times, the artificial beauty wouldn't do her any good. Dana would simply end up looking ridiculous.

As a plain woman, she was best off just accepting her appearance, rather than making a fool of herself trying to improve upon it.

R.J. leaned down to see her face, his brows lowered

slightly in a frown. "You don't like it? You can exchange it for something else…"

Oh, God, she liked it *so* much. "It's…it's beautiful." The words were forced through her tight throat. What did the necklace mean? Anything? Nothing? Would such an exquisite piece of jewelry look out of place on her?

"I noticed the other day that you never wear jewelry," R.J. told her quietly. "Then I saw the necklace, and the emerald is almost the exact shade of your eyes. It's not so fancy that you'd need a special occasion to wear it, and it's delicate—like you."

She stood frozen, her body vibrating with the force of her pounding heart. "It's too much."

He chuckled, pleased—or amused—by her. "Nonsense. I thought it was just right, and I have good taste. Ask anyone."

"Your good taste will be…wasted on me."

R.J. frowned. "What's that supposed to mean, Dana?" When she didn't answer right away, he touched her cheek. "Dana, trust me. The necklace will look perfect on you."

She did trust him, there was no denying that. She gave a small laugh of her own. "I have absolutely no idea what to say."

"You don't have to say anything. Let's put it on you, okay?"

Before she could begin to protest, R.J. had lifted the necklace from where it nestled in the velvet box. He opened the clasp with a sure flick of his fingers, proof positive that he was no stranger to women's jewelry.

He didn't look at her as he reached around her throat to hook it into place, but Dana was painfully aware of his nearness, of his rich, musky male scent, of the heat that seemed to pulse off him in waves, washing over her and making her skin tingle. If she leaned only a scant inch forward, her breasts would brush his hard chest. The knowledge teased and tantalized her.

Remaining still was very, very difficult.

His fingertips brushed her sensitive nape more than she thought should have been necessary as he hooked the necklace. Her eyes closed, and she struggled to regulate her breathing. After spending years dreaming of a moment like this, she had no idea what to think or do.

R.J. lowered his arms and she opened her eyes again. He didn't look at her face, but rather at the small emerald, which lay just below the hollow of her throat. With infinite care he brushed aside the collar of her taupe blouse so that he could view the necklace more clearly. His hands touched her heated skin. One fingertip stroked there, smoothing the gift into place with a tender, almost tentative touch, making her pulse leap. Then his gaze met hers. His gentle breath brushed her temple as he whispered, "It looks beautiful on you."

Beautiful. That was a word that had never been associated with her in any way. Emotions swelled, exploded. Driven by a blind need she'd never experienced before, Dana slid her arms around his neck and hugged herself close to his big body. The sensation of hard muscle against giving softness, male to female, was enough to make her groan out loud. Her belly drew tight, as did her nipples.

She'd meant to thank him, to show her gratitude with a friendly hug. But she made the mistake of raising her face, and she saw his mouth so close to her own.

She kissed him.

CHAPTER THREE

R.J. CAUGHT his breath as Dana's mouth lifted to his with an innocent, instinctive curiosity. She was a very soft, feminine weight in his arms, her scent sweet and warm, unique. His eyes never closed; instead he watched her, saw the excitement on her features, the flush in her cheeks. He was acutely aware of her heartbeat drumming against his chest.

And he was aware of the fullness in his groin.

He couldn't believe Dana Dillinger had given him a hard-on, but there was no denying the truth. He wanted her, and it was only the novelty of the moment, his own enthralled disbelief, that kept him from carrying her to the desk and laying her across it to finish what she had unknowingly started.

Yet all she'd done was give him a chaste schoolgirl's kiss.

Her eyes were closed, and her breath came in ragged pants. She pressed her mouth more firmly against his, and her small hands tangled in the hair at his nape. She gave a soft, hungry groan, a low vibration of sound that proved she was as turned on as he.

The rush of unexpected lust threw him off balance—a

feeling he didn't like and wouldn't accept. R.J. gripped her upper arms and moved her a few inches away, putting necessary space between their bodies. He could feel her trembling, and he could feel the pulsing excitement in his groin. "Dana."

Her lashes slowly lifted at the sound of her name. Almost immediately, she dropped her hands away from his neck with a gasp. Red hot color washed over her pale cheekbones, and she struggled to turn away.

He held tight, refusing to let her hide herself until she explained what had happened—though his body understood very well.

"I…I'm sorry!" She looked mortified, an expression he'd never seen on her face before. Dana was always cool and poised. His hands tightened in automatic reflex, making her wince. *"R.J."*

With a curse, he released her and paced away. Never in his adult life had he felt awkward with a woman. He had a very neatly prescribed place for the women in his life; they were either family, and therefore given his loyalty and protection without qualification, or they were lovers, kept at a distance, meant to share his bed but little else.

And then there was Dana.

He turned back to her, his confusion well hidden. He eyed her averted face. "Dana, are you all right?"

She was rubbing her arms, but stopped the telling motion the second he looked at her. Right before his eyes, her poise appeared like a velvet curtain, masking her dismay. He realized with sudden clarity that her coolness was as much a deliberate facade as his calm, and it enraged him that she could so easily deceive him.

He didn't give a damn how she presented herself to the rest of the world. But for him, he wanted honesty, and nothing held back.

With a patently false smile, she quipped, "I'm fine. Other than being a little embarrassed by my…overenthusiastic show of gratitude. I'm sorry about that."

He narrowed his eyes, watching her every nuance while looking for a chink in the armor. "Why did you kiss me, Dana?"

She looked him straight in the eye and said, "Because you've been so frustrated and withdrawn lately. I only meant to offer a little comfort, but I got carried away." He stared at her, trying to judge the truth of her words, and she waved a dismissive hand. "For heaven's sake, R.J., it was only a tiny kiss, hardly anything to get riled over. I realize I overstepped myself. It won't happen again."

A little kiss? Didn't she realize he was still hard? Her *little* kiss had hit him with incredible impact, and he instinctively rebelled against it. No woman affected him so easily, and certainly not with a chaste peck.

She stood there now, mild as a spring breeze, seemingly unruffled by the experience, and he just didn't know.

But he sure as hell intended to find out.

He stepped toward her, his gaze hard and intent. Her eyes opened, and she started to back up. Just then the phone on her desk rang, giving her a reprieve.

With an apologetic shrug, she turned away. He could have sworn he saw genuine relief in her eyes as she pushed the button on the conference phone. "R.J. Maitland's office. Dana speaking."

"Dana, it's Megan. Put me through to R.J."

R.J. stepped to the desk. "I'm here, Mother."

"I need you to come to my office, R.J. You, too, Dana."

R.J. saw that Dana was still holding herself stiffly, and there was an unnatural bloom of color in her cheeks, proving she wasn't as unaffected by the small kiss as she'd like him to believe. He frowned at the phone. "Now?" The last thing he wanted was to walk away from this situation without resolving things first. *What* things, he wasn't certain, but something had just happened, and he didn't like it worth a damn.

Megan's tone was half amusement, half command. "Are you too busy, son, to spare me a few minutes?"

R.J. glanced at Dana. She returned his look with one of polite inquiry, and he supposed there was little enough left to be said. Whatever reasons she had for kissing him, she had no intention of discussing them now. His interrogation would have to wait. "I can be there in two minutes."

"Excellent." The phone went dead, and both R.J. and Dana continued to stare at each other.

Dana cleared her throat and clasped her hands together. "Any idea what that's all about?"

Slowly he shook his head, still watching her. "Not a clue, but I guess we're going to find out."

He reached for her arm, and Dana quickly grabbed a steno pad and pencil. Since Megan's office was also on the second floor, they reached it only moments later. R.J. drew up short as he saw Chelsea Markum standing impatiently just inside his mother's door. She glanced at him as he entered, and her smile was saccharine sweet.

R.J. noticed Chelsea's eyes were a dark green, but not the clear, guileless green of Dana's. No, Ms. Markum looked devious, and he kept his own expression enigmatic.

Megan Maitland stepped forward with a smile. "We're all meeting in the reception hall."

"We?" He felt Dana standing stiffly beside him, but he had no idea how to reassure her since he hadn't a clue what was going on.

His mother, tall and slender, gave an imperious nod of her head. "I've allowed one reporter, Ms. Markum, and our own press staff to be present." As they started out of the room, R.J. holding her arm and leading the way, Megan added, "Oh, and, dear, Tanya will also be there."

He damn near missed a step. Staring at the top of his mother's regal white head, he wondered what the hell she was up to. Not once had he been able to reach

Tanya, yet his mother had somehow gotten her to attend this impromptu meeting?

With an effort, he kept his tone merely curious. "Care to tell me why, or is this supposed to be some kind of surprise?"

She slanted him a look with her sharp blue eyes. "Oh, you'll be surprised, all right." Tilting her head over her shoulder to see the flagging Ms. Markum, she added, "You, as well, I think."

R.J.'s gaze briefly met Dana's. She was walking beside the reporter, and even now he felt her unerring support, her confidence in him. With a brief shake of his head, he pushed open the reception hall doors and met his ex-lover's startled gaze. Reining in his anger wasn't easy, but he had no doubt that if he displayed his true feelings for Tanya, Ms. Markum would have a field day with it. He wanted his private life to remain as private as possible, which meant he had to conceal his anger behind cold contempt. Tanya received no more than a brief, dismissive glance.

Looking restless and wary, she stood by the end of a long table. She caught her breath as he entered, panic washing over her features until she resembled a cornered animal. With feigned bravado, her gaze left R.J. and focused on Megan. "What's going on here? If you intend to try intimidating me—"

"Not at all," Megan said, her mouth tilted in a small smile. One of the hospital guards stood at the doors, blocking the way. Tanya couldn't have gotten far without causing a real ruckus. "I've decided we should get this entire situation dealt with, one way or another."

Tanya stared at her in wary defiance. "What does that mean? Are you going to try buying me off? Do you plan to offer more for me to walk away than 'Tattle Today TV' offered for me to come forward?"

Over my dead body, R.J. thought, but he didn't need to speak the words. Megan, looking highly insulted, said, "Never," in a tone that had Tanya backing up a step.

Chelsea Markum spoke for the first time. Her voice was shrill with excitement. "I think I should have a cameraman in here if you're—"

"You can either stay or leave, Ms. Markum, but I've had enough of cameras." Megan's voice remained quiet and calm, but there was an underlying steel in her words, and not for the first time R.J. admired this woman who'd overcome a very humble beginning and was now the matriarch of one of Austin's finest families.

Chelsea visibly suppressed her complaints, and instead pulled out a small tape recorder.

"Now then," Megan continued, scanning the audience, "as you are all aware, I've been given temporary custody of the baby. After spending so much time with him, it occurred to me that there's one positive way to identify the baby's mother."

"But *I'm* the baby's mother!" Tanya blustered.

"So you've said. And you've also named R.J. as the father, but I admit I have my doubts. You see, R.J. simply isn't the kind of man who could have done as you've claimed."

"Everyone knows we were lovers!"

Dana's hand settled on R.J.'s biceps. She didn't try to restrain him, which would have been a foolish effort, but her soft touch offered a measure of calm and helped him to maintain his control. He didn't acknowledge her in any way, fearful of the moment being misconstrued. He didn't want Dana drawn into this small war. But he did regain his casual stance, and that reassured her enough that she removed her hand.

"Very well," Megan said, unaware of R.J.'s fury, or else able to completely ignore it. "Since I've had the baby in my home, I've noticed one very obvious clue to his true identity. As his mother, you would immediately know what I'm speaking about, wouldn't you, Tanya? It's hardly something a mother would miss."

R.J., having no idea what his mother was getting at, watched Tanya's face blanch. Knowing Tanya and her conspiring ways, he could tell she was struggling, trying to come up with an answer that would appease everyone. Chelsea Markum hovered nearby, her tape recorder whirring away, her expression rapt.

"This is ridiculous!"

"Not at all, Tanya." Megan began to pace the room, but her gaze never left Tanya. "I think we all agree it's imperative for the baby's sake that we find the truth."

Tanya turned away, her hands fisted. She strode the length of the table, then turned. Finally she cleared her throat. "You're probably referring to the…tiny scratch the baby had on his arm."

Megan smiled, and the look was almost predatory. R.J. felt the first stirrings of satisfaction as he watched his mother in action. Beside him, Dana let out a shaky breath, and he knew she was feeling the same relief. He suddenly wanted to hold her, to take her hand. The idea disquieted him. He didn't need comfort from anyone.

And even if he did, he wouldn't dare touch Dana. The last thing he wanted was to give Chelsea new fodder for her audience, or to accidentally pull Dana into the scandal.

"No," Megan said, "there was no scratch."

"Then you're talking about the baby's…cowlick."

Megan merely shook her head.

Tanya's eyes narrowed as she tried furiously to think of something else, and R.J. made a sound of disgust. "Give it up, Tanya. You know damn well the baby isn't yours—*or mine*."

She flared at him, her chin shooting into the air. "Blue socks. The baby was wearing embroidered blue socks."

Megan's voice sounded almost gentle. "No, Tanya, he wasn't."

Dana gave a loud sigh of relief, moving infinitesimally closer to R.J. Deliberately, he let his arm brush hers, accepting her support. "The world knows you're a liar, Tanya." Then he glared at Chelsea Markum. "Of course, with that damn reward being thrown out there, it was almost a given that someone would crawl out of the woodwork, trying to lay claim."

Chelsea raised an auburn brow. "You're blaming me for this mess?"

"You've played your part in it."

"You know, it occurs to me, Mr. Maitland, that just because Tanya isn't the mother doesn't mean you're not the father."

Every muscle in his body bunched. "What the hell are you talking about now?"

"There was a letter claiming the baby to be a Maitland, don't forget. Everyone saw it, so you're not off the hook yet. As far as I'm concerned, until the real father owns up to his obligations, all the Maitland men are still suspect."

Tanya used the distraction to stalk out of the room. When R.J. noticed her, Megan put a hand on his arm. "She's gone, and good riddance." Then she turned toward Chelsea. "You'll print the truth?"

Chelsea shrugged. "That Tanya was a fraud? Of course. It's a great story. Even though I have to take your word about the so-called identifying clue."

Megan reached over and snapped off the tape recorder. With a glitter in her eyes that spoke volumes, she added, "If you want to continue to have first rights on this story, you'll make certain you print the *exact* truth."

Chelsea bristled. "Are you threatening me?"

R.J. thought she looked titillated by the possibility.

He shared a quick, conspiratorial glance with Dana and almost smiled. They both knew Chelsea was no match for Megan, not when Megan was protecting her own.

Megan shook her head. "Of course not. I'm merely making my position on the matter clear."

Chelsea nodded and took her leave, seeing that all the grand news was over. Megan watched her go with a frown. "That woman is a barracuda."

R.J. stared at his mother, caught in a mix of emotions. In so many ways, he worried about her, especially with all the scandal of late. But every so often she managed to remind him what a strong, capable woman she was. He said simply, "Thank you."

"You're very welcome."

"Why the sudden disclosure?" He was curious about how she could have kept such a "clue" secret for so long, and why. If she'd had proof, why hadn't she used it earlier and spared them all?

Megan reached up for a hug, and R.J. readily indulged her. "I'm sorry," she murmured, leaning back to see his face. "I've been so distracted what with the baby, the clinic's anniversary and then with Connor suddenly showing up…."

R.J. scowled at that reminder. He wasn't too keen on this so-called long-lost cousin. Connor O'Hara had crawled out of the woodwork, and his timing couldn't have been more unfortunate.

"R.J. wasn't blaming you, Megan," Dana offered, automatically stepping in to smooth things over for him.

She did that a lot, too, R.J. realized, kept his life organized and orderly even out of the office. She reminded him of family birthdays and holidays. She sometimes bought the gifts for the occasions, as well. He shook his head in dawning wonder as she added, "He's just been very worried himself."

Megan gave Dana an assessing look. "I trust you're taking very good care of him?"

Dana laughed, but it sounded a bit forced. "I'm doing my best."

R.J. eyed her determined expression, then smiled. "Her best is pretty impressive, as far as I'm concerned." He watched Dana blush as he said it, and knew she was thinking of the simple, sizzling kiss she'd given him. Since he hadn't fully recovered himself, he found it prudent to change the subject. "So, Mother, are you going to tell me what this mysterious clue is?"

Megan's smile turned impish. "I don't believe I will. This is our ace in the hole, possibly the only chance we'll have to sort truth from fiction. The real mother will know what I'm talking about, so it's best if I just keep it to myself."

Now that he was no longer being named the irresponsible father, R.J. didn't care enough to press her on it. Chelsea Markum could still make trouble, just as she'd promised to do. But now that Tanya was discredited, he really had nothing to worry about. He was so relieved to have that worry put to rest, he wanted only to get back to his office with Dana so they could talk.

The anticipation he felt annoyed him, and he forced himself to stay with his mother awhile longer, proving to himself, if no one else, that nothing had actually changed between him and Dana.

Everyone else had left the reception hall, including Maitland's press personnel and the security guard. For the moment, at least, they'd done all they could to suppress the scandal.

Only Megan, Dana and he lingered in the reception hall. "How is Connor settling in?" R.J. asked, trying not to let his suspicions filter through.

Connor claimed to be the son of Clarise Maitland O'Hara, Megan's estranged sister-in-law. Clarise and her husband, Jack, had had a falling out with the family and moved away from Austin a long time ago. There had been no contact between the families over the years, and now that both his parents were dead, Connor had suddenly appeared to mend the long rift.

Megan had welcomed him with open arms, disregarding her children's concern. Still, Connor was one more reason for R.J. to worry about her. Though he'd only met the man briefly, he'd wanted his mother to let him run a check on him, to verify his story, but Megan had insisted on taking care of the matter.

Seeing R.J.'s concern and hearing the words he hadn't spoken, Megan studied her son closely. He was worried about her, she knew, but for the moment, she could do nothing to reassure him. At least not where Connor was concerned. Only her daughter Ellie knew the whole truth about Megan's *nephew,* and Ellie had promised to keep her secret—at least for now.

Eventually she'd have to share the story of her tragic past with all her children, Megan realized. They had a right to know, especially now that she'd found out her baby boy hadn't died when she was seventeen, regardless of the lie her father had told her. Regardless of how they'd all lied to her. Connor was alive, and that was all that mattered—for now.

Standing a little straighter, Megan shook off the heartache of the past. Her family had their hands full tending to the scandal surrounding another boy. Her own past would have to wait. After all, forty-five years had passed, so what would a few more months matter?

Megan summoned her most motherly smile, the one that reminded her children she was perfectly capable of taking care of herself, despite how they liked to fret. "As you know, Connor has moved into one of the family condos. I thought that would be easiest."

Easiest, or cheapest? R.J. wondered, still not liking the situation at all. He rubbed his chin as he watched his mother's expression. "That's…very generous of you."

Megan lifted one brow. "I can afford to be generous, and you know it. Besides, he's family."

"And I suppose you've given him money?"

Her stern expression showed that she considered his question impertinent. "Don't fret over it, R.J. I know what I'm doing. If you recall, I've been handling my own affairs rather well for quite some time now."

With a reluctant grin, R.J. drew her to him for one more hug, then set her away from him. "Of course you have. And now you're handling mine, as well. I hope this newest disclosure about Tanya will stifle some of the speculation. I'm getting damn sick and tired of being gossiped about."

Dana shook her head. "Nothing will stop the gossip completely until the parents are named. You heard Ms. Markum—the Maitland men are still fair game." Her brows drew down, and her slender nose wrinkled. "I wanted to trip her as she left."

Startled, R.J. stared at her a moment then burst out laughing. Megan seemed taken aback by his lack of restraint, then she smiled.

As she started out the door, Megan said, "I have to admit, Dana, the same thought crossed my mind."

R.J. chuckled again.

In some ways, he mused, Megan and Dana had a lot in common. They were both strong, proud women. Strange that he was just now noticing the similarities.

But then, he'd noticed a lot of things about Dana lately. And that, more than anything, made him very determined to get their working relationship back on track.

Two MORNINGS LATER, Dana stepped into the office, early again in the hopes of freeing up some time for R.J. But before she'd even turned the lights on in the dim room, she knew she wasn't alone.

R.J.

She knew it was him. She could detect his hot musky scent, feel the throbbing awareness of his presence. She also felt more, his emotional turbulence, the beat of his anger. What was wrong?

Quickly placing her purse in a file drawer, she rushed across the plush carpet in the outer office to R.J.'s inner sanctum. He sat behind his desk, staring out the window at the early morning traffic on Mayfair Avenue. Bright sunshine flooded through the window and illuminated the office. It reflected off his light brown hair and gilded his brown lashes, leaving shadows on his lean cheekbones.

His mood was disturbing, though he hadn't yet said anything. "R.J.?"

Very slowly he turned his chair to face her.

Since that awkward kiss where she'd made a total fool of herself, he'd been more distantly polite than ever. Dana had gone out of her way to reestablish their professional relationship, burying her feelings deep. R.J. had seemed to welcome her efforts, and returned them in kind.

But now, his eyes burned with a harsh light. "You're early."

"So are you." Dana surveyed his features and then turned briskly to make coffee. "First things first, R.J. I need coffee, and I assume you do, too."

Rather than wait for her, he unfolded himself from

the chair and followed her out. "Thanks. I could use a cup."

Dana looked at him sharply. "Are you all right?"

"Just dandy." He shoved his hands into his pockets and leaned against her desk while she measured coffee and water.

Once she was done and the coffee machine had begun to hiss, Dana turned to him and crossed her arms over her sand-colored suit jacket. "What's wrong?"

R.J. dropped his head forward with a humorless laugh. "Shall I add mind reading to your repertoire of sterling qualities?"

There was more bite in his tone than usual. "It doesn't take a mind reader to know something's upset you. What's happened?"

"Hell, what hasn't happened? This infernal situation has gone from bad to worse."

"You want to explain the *worse* part?"

He gave her a cynical smile. "Sure, why not? Last night, one of our more high-profile mothers checked out of the clinic."

"The movie star?"

"Bingo." He shook his head in disgust. "And right now, three prominent families are packing up to go, too."

"But...I don't understand. I thought since you'd been cleared, everything would have calmed down some. It doesn't make sense that they're leaving now—"

"Nothing has calmed down. Chelsea Markum made

an announcement late last night that they're upping the reward from five thousand dollars to fifty thousand for an exclusive with the real mother. This morning, dozens of women showed up to lay claim to the title."

"Oh my God."

"Damn right." He gave her another cynical smile. "And guess who they're naming as the father."

Dana groped for her chair and then fell into it. "*Dozens* of women?"

"At least forty." R.J. managed a rough laugh. "Hell, I don't know whether I should be insulted or complimented. What kind of a Lothario do they think I am? My social calendar has never been busy enough to accommodate forty women. But does that concern Markum?" He snorted. "Right now, she's interviewing each and every one of them, hoping like hell she can nail me to the wall. We're losing patients because of this publicity. Every paper from the most respected to the worst rags are lobbying out in our parking lot, hounding everyone who goes in or out."

Dana shut her eyes. Several people had approached her when she'd arrived this morning, but at the same time, a limo had pulled up to the curb and drawn them away. She'd thought someone in the limo was checking in, but now wondered if it was someone preparing to pick up a patient and check out—a more likely possibility.

She swallowed hard. "I can't believe all those women are trying to name you—"

"Oh, it's not just my blood they're after. Since Jake isn't around to defend himself, he's become another prime target."

Dana had met Jake Maitland once, but she wasn't sure what he did for a living. She'd heard rumors of him being a government agent of some sort. She knew whatever he did was secretive and kept him away more often than not. "At least they're not singling you out."

"It doesn't matter." R.J. began pacing, his movements agitated and stiff. "All this attention is damaging the clinic and threatening the anniversary party. You know what that party means to my mother."

"Megan can hold her own, R.J." The coffee was ready, and Dana got up to pour R.J. a cup. She handed it to him, and he took several deep gulps before speaking again.

There was a spark of sardonic humor in his eyes as faced her. "You want to know what my mother is doing right now? She's questioning the women."

"Her secret clue?"

R.J. nodded. "So far, the guesses have ranged from webbed feet to mismatched eyes."

"Oh, lord."

"My thoughts exactly. Next thing you know, some ditzy woman will claim the baby has wings."

Dana hid a smile. R.J. could rail and curse and stomp all he wanted, but deep down, he maintained his sense of humor. He might not laugh or joke often, but neither was he an infernal grouch.

And his concern for the baby was evident, despite his frustration. "Maybe Megan will be able to send them all home this afternoon."

"I doubt it. Some of them are refusing to answer her question or even take a guess, claiming it's an insult to the love they feel for the baby, or that the baby's affliction is no one's business."

Dana lifted her brows. "So now the clue is an affliction? I suppose that's as good a cover as any."

"Even if Mother did get them all booted out, more would show up. I have to do something, Dana. I've been totally discredited as far as the public is concerned. First I'm accused of abandoning a defenseless infant, now I've been leaping from one bed to the next at the speed of light." He moved to stand directly in front of her. "All night long, after the 'Tattle Today TV' report, I've been thinking about this. I need to repair the damage done to my name, and hopefully in turn, that'll help the clinic's reputation."

Something in his expression warned her. He was watching her too closely, as if to judge her reaction. He did that often. R.J. was notorious for standing back and absorbing reactions and responses so he could use them to his advantage, a means to an end. It made him an excellent businessman and—by repute—an excellent lover.

She shivered at the thought, then quickly pulled her mind back to the problem at hand.

What could R.J. possibly want from her? Especially

when she'd already promised she'd do anything in her power to help?

Dana sipped her coffee, refusing to be drawn in by his speculative scrutiny. He liked the effect he had on people, how easily he could rattle them, but she refused him the satisfaction of making her squirm. That was one reason she'd lasted so long as his secretary—she pretended to be immune. R.J. needed strong people around him to counteract his autocratic nature. Weaker people got trampled; strong people got his respect. "Do you have any ideas on how to handle this?"

He crossed his arms over his chest and stared down at her, his gaze hard and direct, unrelenting. "Yes. I'm going to get married."

CHAPTER FOUR

THE LOOK on her face wasn't encouraging, R.J. thought. She appeared caught between disbelief, nausea and hysteria. The disbelief he understood perfectly. Dana knew better than most how he felt about marriage.

The nausea and hysteria he hoped were from surprise. *Happy* surprise.

Then that serene curtain dropped over her features and her expression became blank. It annoyed him that she worked so hard to hide her feelings from him, especially now, when he needed to know what she was thinking.

She looked past him, not meeting his eyes. "I see. Are you sure that's the...right move to make?"

Her voice trembled the tiniest bit, and R.J. wondered how best to explain his plan so he could gain her cooperation.

With an edge of steel in his tone, he said, "I don't see too many other options, Dana. I thought about it last night, before Markum even offered the money for the exclusive. If I marry, I'll immediately represent the settled, domestic family man instead of a free-swinging bachelor."

Obviously agitated, she got up to pour herself more coffee. It struck him that they spent a lot more time talking lately than usual. When she'd come in, Dana had set a large stack of files on her desk. Work she'd taken home? His resolve hardened as he considered that possibility.

"Dana, have I put you behind in your work by bringing my personal problems into the office?" He wasn't used to sharing his worries so openly, so he hadn't even noticed the amount of time he'd kept her away from her desk.

She waved the suggestion away. "No, of course not."

She sounded positive, but he couldn't let it go. "You're the most industrious woman I've ever known. I can't remember a time when you haven't filled every available minute with work, but for some time now you've been coddling me while I sit here and grumble."

"That's not true!" Her head lifted with a brief show of temper, ready to defend him—even against himself. "You've had a lot on your mind and I've...I've enjoyed our chats."

He nodded at the stack of files. "Have you been working at home?"

Her expression turned wary. "Just a little."

"Then how have you been keeping up, because I know you too well to think you'd ever let yourself fall behind. You're as conscientious about work as I am."

Her eyes narrowed and her shoulders squared. "If you

must know, I've been coming in earlier, getting things done before you arrive."

"Goddamn it." Filled with disgust for himself, R.J. sighed loudly. "That's what I was afraid of. But it's at an end right now, honey, you understand?"

At the use of the endearment, she froze, and her slender brows shot up a good inch. She turned mute on him, merely staring.

R.J. chuckled. "Well, that certainly got your attention, didn't it?"

"I—"

"No, don't start explaining things to me. I'm sorry if I took you by surprise."

She crossed her arms over her chest and he noticed how the gesture made the bottom of her jacket flare open, displaying the curves of her hips. Damned if he'd ever noticed before that Dana *had* hips! The discovery filled him with disquiet and a simmering curiosity, which he doggedly suppressed. "No more working before or after hours, understood?"

"Whatever you say, R.J."

Which meant she'd do whatever she damn well pleased, R.J. thought. He sighed again in massive frustration, then decided to let it go. After all, if things went according to plan, he'd soon be in a better position to know if she was working more than she should. "I think we need to get back on the topic."

That got her moving. She darted around the office, busying herself with everything and nothing. But instead of her usual smooth movements, every gesture seemed strained and jerky, as if driven by temper.

"Dana, will you settle down? I'm trying to talk to you."

She glanced at him as she bustled past. "About your marriage? Good luck. Oh, and congratulations."

He caught her arm and drew her to a standstill in front of him. "I'm not done explaining."

She glared at him, her eyes every bit as bright as the emerald just visible at her throat. She'd worn the necklace every day since he'd given it to her, and there were times when he wondered if she'd taken it off at all. Picturing it on her while she slept or showered had provided him with a few uncomfortable moments.

"What's to explain? It's an idiotic plan, but then I'm just the secretary, so what do I know?"

Her vehemence took him off guard. When she again tried to pull away, he gently maintained his hold with both hands. "I suspect you have quite a bit to say about it."

"Oh, no, you don't. You're not going to involve me in this farce." She struggled against him again, and when he didn't release her, went back to killing him with her eyes. "You want to marry some bimbo for the sake of your image, that's fine, but don't expect me to give my blessing. That's asking too much!"

He couldn't help but laugh at that, which made her practically growl in response. She looked ready to inflict violence on him.

"Dana... No, just hold still a minute, will you?" As she settled mutinously in his grip, he added, "And please refrain from calling yourself a bimbo. Even if you know something I don't about your character, I'm afraid I can't tolerate that type of insult." He watched her closely as he continued, waiting for her reaction. "Not to my future wife."

He was taking a huge gamble, joking about it that way, but he thought it might make things easier for her if he set the tone up front for what their marriage would be. It wouldn't be a romantic alliance, so he'd be damned if he'd go down on one knee.

Dana became curiously still in front of him. Her eyes were enormous, her brows puckering her forehead with a look of guarded trepidation. "What in the world are you talking about?"

With a subtle pressure, he slid his hands up her arms, attempting to ease her tension. His thumbs settled into the hollows where her shoulders blended into her upper chest. She was so small-boned, his fingers spread easily over her back, nearly covering her shoulder blades. He felt a small quiver go through her and released her.

Apparently she had given up on running from him, so at least he'd get the chance to better explain his intent. He had no doubt he'd get her eventual agreement, but he wanted to make it as easy as possible, to avoid any major conflicts. The truth was, he had no real idea how she'd react.

He spoke in murmuring tones, not wanting her to feel

pushed. "You and I have always understood each other, Dana. We work well together, and in all the years I've known you, we've never had a genuine quarrel."

"That's only because I learned early on how to get around your temper, R.J."

He held his smile in check. "Exactly. You're intelligent, and you're quick." She looked far from complimented by his praise, so he cut to the heart of the matter. "I think we'll suit each other quite well. I need a wife who can counter all this nasty gossip and handle herself well under pressure. I need someone with a respectable background, with no outrageous secrets to uncover. You're quietly elegant, and you have a sophistication all your own."

Dana groped behind her for the desk, and still almost missed it when she went to lean her hip there. R.J. caught her before she could tumble to the floor, then kept one hand on her elbow until she was safely propped on the edge. Still, he stayed close because she didn't look at all steady. It wasn't like Dana to be clumsy, and he chose to see it as a good sign.

R.J. watched her with quiet intent, trying to decipher her thoughts, to gauge his next move. There were a lot of emotions flashing across her face, but gleeful acceptance wasn't one of them.

"Dana?" When her gaze lifted to his, he tried for a reassuring smile. "I realize you might not have been expecting this, but I promise you, I've given it a lot of thought."

She stared at him, not blinking, and a new possibility occurred to him, making him frown. "You're not involved with anyone."

He made it a statement rather than a question. He'd never heard of her seriously dating—hell, he'd never heard of her dating at all. But that didn't mean there wasn't someone hovering on the sidelines, and that possibility made him clench his fists with unwarranted anger. For all he knew, despite her reserved demeanor at work, she could be having a torrid affair with any number of men who—

Without a word, she shook her head, putting his mind, and his temper, at ease.

He told himself he didn't want his plans thwarted, but he knew there was another reason for his relief. Dana had been his for a long time. *His* secretary, *his* friend, *his* confidante. He wasn't a man to share in any way, shape or form. "Good. That's good."

She still hadn't said anything, and annoyance gnawed at the fringes of his good intentions. "I want to assure you that things will go on pretty much as usual, if that's a concern."

One of her brows inched up higher than the other.

"We're friends and we'll remain so, " he went on. "That won't change. You won't be expected to sleep with me. My house is plenty large enough to accommodate two people. You'll have your own room and as much privacy as you might need."

Her look became so incredulous his temper snapped. "You could damn well say something!"

"I…I don't know what to say. You want a…a marriage of convenience?"

Hadn't he made that clear from the start? He gave one brisk nod.

She looked at him with accusation plain in her eyes. "But that's positively archaic!"

He kept his sigh to himself. He didn't understand this new show of temper, when he'd meant to reassure her. "It's a viable solution."

Shaking her head as if in wonder, she carefully edged around him and walked across the office. R.J. allowed her to think things through for a few minutes, forcing himself into an unaccustomed patience. Generally when he wanted something, he went after it with single-minded determination. This marriage was no different.

She kept pacing, and the silence got to him. "How old are you, Dana?"

She barely glanced at him, lost in her contemplation. "Twenty-nine."

Even though Dana had been friends with his sister forever, R.J. realized he knew little about her personal life. He frowned. "Have you ever been married?"

She cast him a worried glance. "No."

"Engaged?"

"No."

He nodded in satisfaction—and mingled relief.

"That's what I thought. It's obvious to me that you're not some romantic dreamer who's waiting for a knight in shining armor to come along and put stars in your eyes. You're rock solid—"

"Be still my heart."

"—and mature and reasonable."

"Gosh, you make me sound just lovely. Like a decrepit old spinster."

She drew closer and he caught her, forcing her to look at him. He cupped her face, ignoring her sudden breathless reaction to his touch and his nearness.

Given the way he'd sprung things on her, she was justifiably on edge. He didn't mind her honest reaction, but he refused to let her shut him out. "Dana, honey, I don't mean to make those attributes sound like insults. The truth is, I like you a lot. There aren't many women I'd make such a proposition to."

"Uh-huh." She didn't look at all convinced. "You do mean proposal, don't you?"

"Semantics." His fingertips were in her hair, and he felt its softness, its warmth, without disturbing the careful arrangement. Again, he wondered about her hair, how it would look loose. As soon as they were married, that was one curiosity he'd put to rest. "I'm talking about a business arrangement. As my wife, new doors will open for you."

"I don't need any doors opened," she said quietly.

"Your life will be easier," he argued. "You wouldn't have to work if you didn't want to—"

"Whoa, just a minute."

Again she stepped out of his reach, moving a good two yards away then turning to face him. Her cheeks were bright red, but her eyes were direct and resolute, her shoulders squared as if for battle. R.J. thought she would refuse him, and already he was forming arguments to sway her to his way of thinking. She should know him well enough to realize he didn't give up his goals easily. She must also realize that a wife would be the most expedient way to repair his reputation.

And he hadn't lied to her; in fact, she was the *only* woman he'd be willing to make such an alliance with.

"First," she said, raising one finger in an imperious manner fit for a queen, "I'm going to work. There's no way I want someone else financially responsible for me."

His stomach muscles tensed as the meaning behind her words kicked in. *She was going to agree.* All that was left was the negotiation, and he had no doubt that would go his way. He struggled to keep his satisfaction hidden, not wanting to give her more reasons for anger. If she knew how triumphant he felt right now, she probably wouldn't like it.

However, he couldn't do a damn thing about his small smile.

"If you want to work, that's fine," R.J. murmured. He really didn't care one way or the other, but he hoped to change her mind once they were wed. As he'd explained, the marriage would be a business agreement, and he'd owe her for agreeing to it. Giving her some much-needed time away from work seemed like the perfect start to him. Dana had taken few vacations over the years, and to his knowledge, she'd never traveled far. She deserved to go anywhere she liked, maybe to Paris or New Orleans. And he'd gladly fund the trip. Or perhaps she'd like to buy herself more emeralds.

Strangely enough, he could easily picture her decked solely in emeralds, and the image was decidedly erotic. He would, he decided, make the arrangement for more jewelry himself.

He shook his head to clear it. "I knew you'd be reasonable about this."

"Don't get too cocky yet until you've finished hearing me out."

"More stipulations?" he asked, prepared to be indulgent. The color in her cheeks intensified, and he could see how difficult it was for her to maintain eye contact. Curiosity swamped him. What would she ask for? A new car? An expense account? He could easily afford either, so he waved away her concerns. "This isn't necessary, you know. I'm more than willing to give you whatever you need."

She drew a long, shaky breath and visibly braced herself. "I'm glad to hear you say that, R.J.—because what I want is a real marriage."

He took exception to her insinuation and with deadly calm explained, "Oh, it'll be real, all right, you don't have to worry about that. We'll be legally wed. I wouldn't ask you to do anything unethical—"

"You're not paying attention, R.J." She drew another breath and blurted, "I want sex."

Everything in him seemed to shudder and stall, then kicked into overdrive until his body fairly hummed with his racing pulse. Exercising extreme politeness, he whispered, "Excuse me?"

Her face was so red it was almost comical, only he had absolutely no desire to laugh. He felt the tension in the air, and the even more palpable tension in Dana. He waited in silence while she worked out her thoughts.

"I want us to be a regular married couple," she explained softly. "I want intimacy."

His eyes narrowed the tiniest bit, and she continued, her tone a bit forced, but filled with resolve. "I'm talking about the same bedroom, R.J., the same bed, every night. If I'm going to be married to you for however long it takes to repair the damage to the clinic and your own reputation, then I expect to be treated like a wife during that time—with all the privileges due a wife."

He stared at her, still trying to figure out how he was misunderstanding, because he was certain he couldn't be hearing her right.

She made a broad, nervous gesture with her hands. "Don't get me wrong, R.J. I'll do anything I can to help. Though I'm not sure marrying me will really improve your image, I'm willing to give it a try. We can have a few cocktail parties, get involved in some community activities, become the epitome of marital bliss for the media. Whatever it takes, whatever you want. I'll do anything you think will help. But in return, I want—"

"Sex," he finished for her, the single word laced with ice. "You're standing there demanding sex."

"With you," she clarified shakily, on the off chance he hadn't realized that much.

With a slow, measured stride, he stalked forward to close the space between them. "What game are you playing, Dana?"

She looked as though she wanted to retreat, but instead, she dug in, facing him squarely. "No game."

He gripped her shoulders and shook her slightly. It seemed he'd touched her more in the past week than in all the previous years combined. "Honey, I know you too well to buy this. Since when have you become so sexual? I've never even heard you say the word before now."

She appeared to resent that. Some of her embarrassment faded, and indignation took its place. "I'm as sexual as the next woman!"

He flicked the top button of her suit coat. "Yeah, right. You dress like a nun and you never date. When was the last time you had an affair? When was the last time you even had sex?" Her face paled, but he pressed on. "When was it, Dana?"

"That's none of your business." She trembled all over, and then abruptly turned away. "Just forget about it.

If it's too much to ask, if it's a *hardship,* then there's nothing more to talk about."

R.J. pulled back, watching her walk stiffly away. He didn't mind her anger. In fact, he'd set out to provoke it, preferring her anger over her insistence that he make love with her. But watching her retreat, he realized he'd gone too far.

It was obvious he'd hurt her feelings, and he wanted to kick his own ass. Things had seemed much more straightforward when he'd first come up with this plan. "Dana." She didn't look up. "I never said it would be a hardship."

The look she shot his way should have left him bleeding profusely on the floor. She threw herself into her chair and snapped open a file as if ready to forget the entire thing.

He couldn't let her do that.

Then he noticed her hands were shaking and her breath was catching in tiny pants. Good Lord, was she going to cry? Because she wanted to have sex with him and he'd pretty much refused? It boggled the mind. Of all the possible scenarios he'd figured might accompany his proposition, this particular one had never come up.

He went to her desk and sat on the edge. "Dana, you're a friend, sweetheart. That's all I meant." She didn't look the least bit appeased, and he floundered. He'd spoken the truth when he said sleeping with her wouldn't be a problem. Just the opposite, in fact. He was afraid he'd enjoy it far too much. That one simple kiss they'd shared had plagued his mind ever since, waking him too often in the middle of the night.

If he made love to her, nothing would ever be the same again.

Yet he'd always valued her so much as a friend, as a confidante. Her intelligence and kindness and loyalty had set her apart from other women, and he knew in his heart that once they'd given in to lust, their relationship would be irreparably altered. The qualities of their friendship that he valued most, the ones that had made the plan seem so ideal, might cease to exist. Sex had a way of muddying the waters, especially with a woman like Dana, a woman who didn't take physical relationships lightly.

He'd always gravitated to women who knew the score and expected nothing more from him than a good time in and out of bed. When he was with a woman, he treated her well, indulged her with expensive gifts and flattery. But that was as far as it went. When he tired of her company, or if she got too clingy, he moved on. He left himself free to do just that.

He didn't have to worry about forsaking his obligations, as his father had done, because he made sure there were none.

Tanya had tried to wheedle him into marriage, but he'd refused to allow her the upper hand. For some reason she'd thought she was special, though he'd been upfront with her from the start—as he always was. She hadn't agreed to go away easily. It had cost him an expensive gift to soften the blow, one she'd accepted with ill grace.

At the time, he'd considered the price little enough to pay. He'd appeased his sense of fair play, and still remained free.

Marrying for the sake of his reputation didn't put him at risk. He wasn't expected to offer love everlasting, and he wouldn't be obliged to start a family.

But if Dana expected a real marriage, that would change everything. What if it turned out he was more like his father than he thought?

"R.J.? I have a question."

Her tone sounded reasonable enough. Which he considered good cause for worry. "Go ahead."

"How long, exactly, do you expect this marriage to last?"

"There's no way I can predict that, Dana." And if he was truthful with himself, even trying to speculate on an answer was a lesson in keen frustration. Right now, he had all the frustration he could stand.

"But you do have a certain term in mind, don't you?" Her eyes were narrowed again, making the green brighter, more intense. Her pen tapped against the desktop. "Do you think things can be repaired in a week, a month, six months?"

He pushed away from the desk with repressed anger. "How the hell should I know? It took little enough time to destroy my reputation, but somehow I think it'll take considerably longer to mend it."

"You're probably right." Her gaze stayed glued to him as he strode across the room. "Which brings up another interesting thought. Do you plan to stay celibate during our marriage, or am I simply supposed to look the other way?"

He whirled to face her, thoroughly insulted at such a suggestion. "Being an adulterer would hardly improve my image."

"Oh? Then you do intend to remain celibate, even if it takes a year."

"I—" The protest died before it was spoken. He actually hadn't thought his plan through that far, so how could he take offense at her presumption that he wouldn't honor his wedding vows? When he'd come up with the idea to marry, it had been a near desperate decision. Though he didn't want the world to know it, it ate him up inside that the residents of Austin were beginning to see him as indulgent and reprehensible, an immoral reprobate who would blithely walk away from a woman carrying his child. The image sickened him and dredged up old feelings left over from childhood, from knowing his father hadn't cared enough, hadn't been responsible enough to fulfill even the smallest obligations to his children.

The turbulent memories were swept away as Dana once again stood, very slowly, to face him. "I've always known I was a plain woman."

R.J. glared at her. "What are you talking about?"

"It's just occurred to me. You don't want to sleep with me for the same reason you chose me to proposition."

He didn't like her tone or the direction of her thoughts. "Propose to."

Her grin was tight as she mimicked him by saying, "Semantics." She stalked out from behind her desk. "There must be any number of women who'd jump at a chance like this. Even if the marriage only lasted a few weeks, as you say, the prestige exists. And everyone knows how generous you are. But then, most of the women you associate with are beautiful and sexy, and that might only reinforce your present image as a man who cares about superficial things and his own pleasure. If you marry me, a woman without extravagant looks or sex appeal and with an unremarkable background, they'll think it has to be for love, the kind of love that lasts."

"The *real* kind."

She totally missed his sarcasm. "You, on the other hand, have looks and money and breeding and background and sophistication. But my drabness will help to tone down your brilliance by comparison. That's it, isn't it?"

He stared at her, totally floored that she would come to such an asinine conclusion when those thoughts had never entered into his decision. "That analogy is a pretty good stretch, wouldn't you say?"

She shook her head, convincing herself she was on

the right track. "I suppose it does make a bit of sense when you think about it. You can't exactly be seen as a playboy married to *me*. No one will wonder if you married me for connections, or money, because I have none."

"You have something much more valuable."

She quirked a dubious brow.

"You have a quiet dignity. And a generous soul, and an innate kindness. Those are all things that will reflect on my good judgment." And she was the only woman he could consider letting that close.

She sighed, then rubbed her forehead. "I do understand, R.J. But it's up to you. Will I be a real wife or not?"

She had no intention of backing down, he could see that now. She stood there in her innocence and naïveté and demanded that he have sex with her. Fighting for lost control, he nodded. "All right, Dana, you win."

Once she had her agreement, she seemed to wither before him. Her eyes were downcast, and she nibbled on her bottom lip. "Are you sure?"

"Having second thoughts now?"

"No. I just…I don't want you to be angry."

Hell, he was far from angry. Turned on, maybe. His body had started to thrum quietly the minute she'd made her outrageous suggestion, and with each second the feeling had only gotten worse. The miracle would be keeping himself detached when they did have sex—but he knew he had to. He would maintain the upper hand, no matter what it took. "I'm not angry."

"Shall...shall I make the arrangements?"

One side of his mouth kicked up in humor as he registered the irony of her question. "The efficient secretary to the last, hmm? Still willing to handle all my affairs, even the more personal ones. Well, I think this time I'll arrange things myself. How does this weekend suit you?"

"So soon?" She couldn't hide her amazement—or her excitement. At least, he hoped it was excitement and not anxiety.

Very gently, he asked, "There's no reason to put it off, is there?"

"But...should I invite someone to be a witness?"

He enjoyed seeing her act like a nervous bride, which proved just how perverse he could be. "Of course. But I'd really like to keep it low key. My mother, two witnesses, but no more than that. I don't want the press to find out until it's over with."

She shuddered at the possibility. "They'd definitely taint the ceremony."

"And I've seen my face enough in the papers lately."

Her eyes widened. "I'll have to find a dress!"

Such a typically female consideration was a relief after her bout of sensual demands. "Your white suit will do just fine. After all, it'll be a civil ceremony at the justice of the peace. And we'll want to keep the frills to a minimum."

The second he said it, he saw a small light go out in her eyes and belatedly realized that she'd wanted to make the occasion special. He had a sudden pang in his chest that he didn't understand, an ache that was unfamiliar but that he knew was centered around Dana and her happiness. He cupped her face with one hand, letting his thumb smooth over her temple. Now that he'd gotten used to touching her, he couldn't seem to stop. Her skin was so incredibly soft. "I'm sorry, sweetheart. Here I am, bulldozing right over you with no consideration for your wishes."

She shrugged, staring at his silk tie. "It was your idea, after all. You should certainly do things however you like."

He frowned. "There's no need for you to play the martyr."

"I wasn't!"

He shushed her by placing his thumb over her lips, which were even softer than her skin, prompting him to continue touching. She froze, her eyes huge. "What I'd like," he murmured, "is to make you happy. If you really want to wear a new dress—"

When she shook her head, he reluctantly removed his thumb so she could speak. "No, the suit will do. You're right."

He hesitated, not wanting her to look so fatally resigned. But he knew that the less fanfare the better—for his reputation and his peace of mind. He already felt far too involved. To make it up to her, he would buy her flowers, traditional white rosebuds to go with the suit. And another emerald for her wedding band. Knowing Dana, she wouldn't be expecting a ring; she wouldn't be expecting anything at all. He didn't want their bargain to be one-sided. He wanted to pamper her and he wanted to see her smile.

But he also wanted to protect himself, because he had a feeling he'd miscalculated his reaction to Dana Dillinger. She'd changed things around so that now it was a marriage of *her* convenience. Her *sexual* convenience. And now that she'd insisted on getting down and dirty with him, he felt thrown off balance in a way he'd never experienced before.

He wanted her. And that had never been part of the plan.

CHAPTER FIVE

"HI, SWEETHEART."

Dana caught her breath as R.J. gently touched her cheek, drawing her attention. She'd been so preoccupied and nervous over the coming ceremony that she hadn't heard him enter. And this new habit of his of using endearments continually caught her off guard. She wondered if she'd ever get used to it.

His smile was teasing, as if he knew she was nervous and found it endearing. "This is for you."

Dana stared down at the large, square white box R.J. handed to her. She'd been surprised by the appearance of the judge's chambers moments before when she and her good friend Hope Logan had arrived. The large room had been fancied up with white satin ribbon and a white runner. And there were flowers everywhere, flanking a small altar, situated on either side of the door, in a row of pots bordering the floor and in every corner. The air smelled sweet with the combined scents of orange blossom, roses, carnations and orchids.

She wasn't sure what she'd expected, but it hadn't been wedding decorations, not when the wedding wasn't real, not when there was no love involved. Hope, one of her closest friends and the only witness Dana had invited to the wedding, had known for some time how Dana felt about R.J. Trusting her friend completely, Dana had confided R.J.'s motive for the wedding, and had been grateful that Hope hadn't tried to dissuade her from going through with it.

When they'd discovered the decorated chambers, Hope had squeezed her hand and whispered, "Dana, you know R.J. doesn't do anything halfway. You probably should have expected this." But she hadn't.

And now R.J. had another surprise for her.

Dana blinked at the box. "What is it?"

R.J. grinned and she privately thought he was the most charming, handsome man she'd ever seen. He looked stunning in his dark suit and white shirt, and there was a white rosebud in his lapel. "I promise you'll find out if you open the box."

Very aware of everyone looking at her with expectation, Dana lifted the lid on the cardboard box and carefully pulled apart tissue paper. Quietly she caught her breath. Lush, fully bloomed, creamy white roses and rosebuds, baby's breath and delicate orchids were framed by intricate white lace and long, dangling ribbons.

He'd bought her a wedding bouquet.

Tears threatened, and she struggled to subdue them. Ever since he'd made his proposition, her emotions had been on a roller coaster ride, winging high with excitement and an irrepressible, ridiculous hope, then soaring to the depths with stark reality. This was all for show, a complete sham. She wondered why everyone smiled. Did they truly not know? R.J. had always had his pick of beautiful women; why would any sane person believe he'd marry her for love?

Faint music started, startling her anew, and R.J. took her arm to turn her toward the altar. The judge stood in front of it, his face alight with pleasure. Hope had taken her place to the right of the judge, smiling despite the fact she knew this was all contrived.

Drake Logan, Hope's husband and R.J.'s good friend, stood to the left of the judge. Megan stood beside Hope, and Dana realized they all had flowers now. Hope and Megan wore corsages that matched her bouquet, and a white rosebud was tucked in Drake's lapel. Why had R.J. gone to all this trouble? Dana wondered.

But, of course, Hope had been right. When R.J. did something, he did it right, with no room for chance. He wouldn't want any speculation about the authenticity of the wedding.

"You're not going to faint on me, are you?" R.J. whispered in her ear as he gently urged her forward.

Numbly, she shook her head, though fainting seemed a very real possibility. "I'm fine."

He chuckled and gave her hand a squeeze. "A typical answer for you. Tell me, do you ever complain about anything?"

The question startled her. "Why would I complain to you? You're my boss, not my counselor or therapist."

"I thought I was your friend, as well."

They were keeping their voices low, barely audible over the music. Dana nodded. "A friend, but one with limitations."

His eyes glittered down at her. "I'm soon to be your husband."

Unable to hide her feelings, she gave him a stark look. "Not really." By this time they had reached the judge, who started in with the prescribed ceremony. Dana could feel the heat of R.J.'s annoyance beside her, but she refused to let herself be deluded. This wedding was meant to repair his reputation, nothing more. His gestures with the flowers and music were appreciated, but then, R.J. was always considerate of the women he associated with. His generosity was well known, but a smart woman understood that it didn't represent anything beyond superficial affection and a desire to please at best, an intelligent tactic at worst. Either way, it was a long, long stretch from love.

"If you don't answer him, sweetheart, I'm going to be mortified."

She heard the teasing in R.J.'s tone and saw the amusement on everyone's face. Her cheeks heated. She'd been so lost in thought she hadn't even heard the question. But the judge was looking at her expectantly, and she knew the appropriate answer. "Yes."

R.J. gave a rumbling chuckle and again squeezed her hand. In an aside to their small audience, he said, "I see she knows how to keep a man on pins and needles," and they all laughed softly. Dana forced a smile, but it fell away with a gasp when R.J. lifted her left hand and slid a wedding band into place on the third finger.

The ring was a narrow, polished gold circle with a glowing emerald embedded in the middle and surrounded by glittering diamonds. Though it was larger and somewhat more extravagant, it matched the necklace to perfection and left her utterly speechless. She stared at it, with no idea what to say.

Not once had she considered the idea of a ring. Her thoughts had centered on maintaining some sort of emotional balance, of taking advantage of the opportunity to be with R.J., to openly love him, without tossing away her pride by letting him discover her love. She had to protect her heart and at the same time feed the growing need to be with him, to touch him, to have all of him—even under false pretenses.

There'd been no room in her thoughts for the formalities of the wedding. R.J. had said to leave it up to him, and she had.

Hope and Megan oohed over the ring, leaning closer to see it better. Drake gave a masculine murmur of approval, prompting Dana to say simply, and somewhat breathlessly, "Thank you."

She hoped everyone would attribute her preoccupation to bridal jitters. R.J. had orchestrated such a convincing facade. He'd manipulated them all so skillfully, playing the doting bridegroom with the flowers and the music and the ring. Only Hope knew that beneath it all, Dana's heart was breaking.

Everything about the wedding shone—except the bride. When Hope had picked her up to bring her to the courthouse, Dana had wanted to run back inside and change. Her white suit, which R.J. had suggested was perfectly suitable seemed dowdy in comparison to Hope's classy silk sheath and pearls. But of course, she'd had nothing more appropriate to change into, only more suits and her casual clothes.

But now her businesslike outfit looked even more utilitarian against the beautiful flowers and the emerald ring. She wanted to shout her frustration, she wanted to run away. *She wanted R.J. to love her.*

And the judge, with a hearty smile, announced, "You may kiss the bride."

Dana sucked in her breath and held very, very still. She felt all the eyes watching her, Hope's with a sort of wistful expectation, Megan's with joy, Drake's mildly amused.

Her thoughts and feelings fractured as R.J. smiled at her. His rough fingertips, so warm and steady, touched her chin, tipping up her face. The worries that had overwhelmed her only seconds before disappeared at the prospect of kissing him again.

Dana forgot to breathe. The kiss wasn't voracious, but rather respectful and restrained. Through the ringing in her ears, she vaguely heard Drake encouraging R.J. to do better, and before she knew it, his mouth was back with new intent.

His hand slid from its gentle touch on her chin to grip

LORI FOSTER 85

the back of her neck and to the sounds of loud cheering, he tilted her over his arm and continued the kiss. Dana could do little more than hang on to his lapels, inadvertently crushing his boutonniere and dropping her bouquet to the floor, as his tongue stroked hers. She actually felt dizzy, and when he lifted his mouth, it was to grin down at her as she remained balanced in his grasp.

Against her lips, he whispered, "Smile, or they'll all think I'm blackmailing you into this."

Smiling was totally beyond her capabilities. Instead, she leaned up the scant inch necessary and brought their mouths together again.

Drake laughed out loud, and Hope and Megan applauded.

Dana was dimly aware of a flash of light, then another. In fact, there had been flashes all through the short ceremony, she realized. R.J. released her mouth and gently drew her upright, then placed one muscular arm around her shoulders. Hope, having rescued the bouquet before it got trampled, handed it to Dana, and they turned to face the photographer.

A small woman with short, straight blond hair and a Bohemian style wielded her camera like a weapon, turning this way and that with an excess of energy. R.J. didn't seem to mind, so Dana assumed this was another surprise, freezing the moment for posterity. She shuddered.

He had joked about the others thinking he'd black-mailed her, when in truth, she was the blackmailer.

And he was paying her demands. She'd insisted he give her all the benefits of a real wife, and evidently he was determined to do just that.

R.J. raised a hand and announced to the group, "Dana and I have arranged a celebration dinner and we insist you all join us, to allow us to show our appreciation."

Dana almost groaned. She wouldn't be able to swallow a bite, and she wanted this over with so she could relax. Then she realized where her thoughts had taken her. Once the celebration was over, they'd be alone—and R.J. would have to pay up, so to speak. She shuddered again at her own daring.

Among the murmur of agreements, R.J. leaned down and kissed her cheek, then whispered in her ear, "This will be the perfect time for our marriage to be leaked to the media. People will see us there, and it'll be reported. That way we won't have to break the news."

"I see."

He turned her to face him, still leaning close, holding her in a loose embrace. She knew it was for the sake of their audience and wanted to pull away. "Does that idea distress you?"

"No, of course not. I want to do whatever you think is best, R.J."

For some reason, her reply seemed to annoy him. Then his frown lifted, replaced by a look of chagrin. "You're not enjoying yourself at all, are you?"

She could tell the idea disappointed him. He'd gone out of his way to make things nice for her, and she was acting like an ungrateful wretch. Luckily the others were all standing a discreet distance away, giving them the privacy they needed. Dana tried to inch back, putting some space between them, and R.J. tightened his hold. She gave up. "Everything is lovely."

He searched her face. "If you're nervous about tonight—"

"No! I mean..." She glanced around. "I don't want to talk about that." Planning it in advance had been so much easier than dealing with it in the present.

He grinned, and then treated her to a swift, hard kiss on her lips. "You can still back out if you want, you know. I won't become a demanding husband."

He held her so close, the only way to avoid his gaze was to drop her forehead against his chest. And that treated her to the scent of his warm body and spicy cologne, the feel of his hard muscles and the rhythmic thumping of his heart. *God, she wanted him.* "I... I haven't changed my mind."

She felt his sigh against the top of her head, his hands coasting gently up and down her spine. "You are a determined woman, aren't you?"

There was no discernible inflection in his tone, which gave her pause. "Does that bother you, R.J.?"

His tight squeeze made her gasp. "Not at all," he said, without an ounce of conviction. "I just hope you know what the hell you're doing."

He stepped away from her, and they went about the formality of signing papers and discussing transportation. R.J. had rented a limo to take them all to the restaurant, and it was waiting in front of the courthouse when they exited. Dana assumed this was another measure to make certain the public took note of the wedding. And sure enough, speculation was rife as onlookers watched the small procession climb into the shining limousine.

R.J. seated Dana in the very back beside him, while Megan sat in the long seat to their right, Drake and Hope to their left. The privacy window was up, so the driver was invisible. Soft music played, and the leather seats creaked as everyone shifted to get comfortable.

"Drake, if you'll do the honors, the champagne is right beside you."

Without a word, the driver pulled away from the curb and Drake retrieved the champagne from the ice bucket and went about filling glasses. When he was through, R.J. lifted his glass in a salute. Smiling at Dana, he said, "To my very special bride."

There was a heartfelt round of "hear, hear," and then everyone drank a toast to Dana.

Megan watched her son and his new bride. She still hadn't quite figured out how this had all come about, but she couldn't have been more pleased. R.J. was a recluse in many ways, so determined to prove himself, though it wasn't necessary at all. He'd become a total workaholic over the years, and her mother's intuition had often told her Dana was the right woman for him, maybe the only woman for him. Dana could stand up to him, meet him eye to eye, where others wouldn't dare. She supported him and believed in him even when he didn't believe in himself. Dana loved him unconditionally.

But R.J. had never seemed to realize it.

Megan had known for some time how Dana felt, though Dana didn't go about sharing that news with just anyone. But the people who knew her well could tell; it was there in the way she looked at R.J., the extreme effort she put out to be totally professional with him at all times. Like a drunk who carefully enunciates in an effort not to give himself away.

The horrid scandal with the baby had been hardest on R.J., and Megan couldn't help worrying about her son. Maybe, just maybe, Dana would be able to save him.

She tilted her head, smiling at them both. "I'm still amazed at how sudden this has been. Honestly, I'd suspected all along there might be more to your relationship than mere business, especially the way Dana has always been able to read you and manage your nasty temper. But marriage?"

Dana blinked, as if surprised by Megan's words, then she blushed. Megan's speculation doubled—and so did her satisfaction. She'd be willing to bet her son had met his match. "I swear, R.J.," she added, deliberately teasing, "I never thought to live to see the day. Dana must be a miracle worker."

Dana thought about sinking beneath the limo seat and hiding. Did Megan know what was going on?

Had R.J. told her, despite his assurance that no one would know?

R.J. merely chuckled while Dana's face grew hot. He was sitting so close beside her in the plush seat, his hard thigh lying alongside her own, his muscled left arm draped around her shoulders.

He tugged her close, almost making her spill her champagne with clumsy nervousness. "There's not another woman in the world I'd have married."

"Then I'm doubly glad to have Dana around," his mother replied.

Dana had a horrible suspicion that they'd both been telling the truth. R.J. had told her many times that he wouldn't have propositioned any other woman, and Megan had never made a secret of her affection. Dana knew Megan liked her, and the feeling was well returned. R.J.'s mother was so different from her own mother, so lively and filled with laughter.

She shook off the disturbing comparison. The last thing she wanted to think about right now was her mother and her lifelong disapproval of her only daughter. But at the same time, Dana hated duping Megan. The woman deserved better from them both.

"Drake," R.J. said, "Next to the champagne there are some gifts I picked up for everyone. Would you pass them over to me, please?"

Surprised, Drake glanced around and located the tray of small packages. He handed it to R.J. with a grin. "I think I like this best man business."

R.J. laughed. "Then by all means, you should go first. Here, this one is for you." Drake took the package, and R.J. turned to the others. "Mother and Hope."

Drake opened his gift without hesitation, then whistled under his breath at the diamond tie clip. "Very nice! Thank you."

"Oh my!" Hope exclaimed when she opened her gift. "R.J., thank you, it's lovely." She held the small gold charm bracelet up for everyone to see. The charm, a golden rose, had a diamond set in the very center.

Megan shook her head. "You are outrageous, R.J. Now, let's see what you got me—oh, goodness. It's lovely, son." She lifted out the elegant diamond stick pin for everyone to see.

R.J. still held one box, and he pressed it into Dana's hand. "A wedding gift, sweetheart."

Dana swallowed nervously. This entire day seemed magical, and if any part of it had been real she'd be the happiest woman alive. Instead, she felt slightly hollow, as if she herself was a sham.

But she was also filled with expectation for the coming night. Conflicting, volatile emotions that made her feel totally off balance.

Her fingers shook horribly as she tore away the silver tissue paper. When she hesitated, R.J. sighed and took the long velvet box from her and carefully opened the hinged top so that Dana could see inside.

This time, the tears almost got her as she glimpsed the emerald bracelet. With a gasp, she launched herself at R.J., making him laugh and gather her close. Likely he assumed it was the costliness of the gift that had so pleased her, but her response had nothing to do with money, and his next words made her chest tighten with the effort to choke back her tears.

To the onlookers R.J. said, "I noticed earlier in the week that Dana looked very fine in emeralds. The color suits her. They perfectly match her eyes."

He didn't think she was too plain to wear such extravagant jewelry.

Dana continued to hide against his shoulder, then she got control of herself and pushed away. She would not continue acting like a complete ninny. One tear slipped down her cheek when she blinked.

Drake gallantly handed her a hanky, which made everyone chuckle again. "I'm sorry," Dana said as R.J. took the hanky from her and tenderly dried her eyes. "I don't know why I'm acting so absurd today—"

"Women are supposed to cry at weddings, silly, even their own!" Hope assured her, then dabbed at her own eyes.

Dana lifted the bracelet from the box. "This is so… so beautiful." She turned to R.J. "Will you help me put it on?"

He touched his mouth to hers in the lightest of kisses, but the emotional impact on Dana was almost more devastating than his blatant performance at the altar. She mustered a shaky smile, which he returned, then he deftly hooked the bracelet around her wrist. Unlike the pendant and ring, which each boasted a single emerald, the bracelet was a multitude of perfect square stones hooked together with gold links. Surprisingly, it wasn't heavy or too ostentatious, and it complemented the other pieces perfectly.

Dana met his warm gaze. "I didn't get you anything." Given his reasons for marrying her, a gift had seemed out of place.

"You married me, sweetheart. Believe me, that's all I need."

Hope and Megan positively cooed, but Dana, determined to be more herself, snorted good-naturedly and poked him in the ribs. "You don't do humble worth a damn, R.J."

R.J. laughed and gave her another hug. Dana was stunned by how much physical affection he was showing her, but she assumed it was expected from a devoted groom on his wedding day.

"You may not be humble," Drake remarked as he surveyed his tie clip, "but you sure as hell know how to do it up right, don't you?"

"Small gestures, that's all. Dana and I appreciate the show of support, especially in light of all that's going on right now."

Hope leaned forward to touch R.J.'s arm. "That mess has nothing to do with you, R.J. We know that."

Drake shook his head. "It is a mess, though, isn't it? Who the hell could have abandoned the baby? And that damn 'Tattle Today' broad. She drives me nuts the way she fans the flames to make a more sensational story and improve ratings."

Megan sighed. "Did you know Lana has been bringing the baby a gift every day? And Michael can't even bear to look at the child. This is so hard on all of them, Shelby and Garrett, too, knowing that they were once abandoned themselves."

Dana knew about R.J.'s "cousins" and their past. The four siblings had been dropped off at Maitland Maternity shortly after it opened. No one had ever returned to claim them. Megan had found a wonderful home for them with good friends of hers, the Lords, and the children had been raised well. But Dana supposed being abandoned wasn't something you'd easily forget.

She looked at R.J. and wondered what he was thinking. He'd been accused of abandoning a baby himself. R.J. was close to the Lords and knew they still struggled with their past. Because of his own father's desertion, his sympathy for them ran deep, and made even the suggestion that he would inflict the same pain on a child doubly hurtful. R.J. would never admit just how much the accusation had affected him, though. He'd stomp about and growl and put on a show of anger, but deep inside, Dana knew he was aching.

R.J. noticed her watching him and took her hand, though it was Megan he spoke to. "There haven't been any dull moments lately, that's for sure."

"You're the master of understatement." Drake settled back in his seat and lifted his champagne once more.

"Enough of that." Megan spoke with brisk command. "This is a day for celebration. There's no reason for us to dwell on all that unpleasantness. Let's change the subject, shall we?"

Dana noticed how R.J. suddenly focused on his mother, his gaze growing intent and purposeful. "All right, Mother. I have a topic for you. Connor."

Megan gave a look heavenward. "What would you like to know, R.J.?"

"Oh, I don't know. Anything. Everything. I'm sure the man has been fascinating since he's shown up."

The look Megan sent her son would have quelled most men. She plainly didn't appreciate his sarcasm one whit. But Dana saw that R.J. wouldn't back down. He was worried about his mother, and that was enough reason for him to butt in.

Megan needlessly twitched the skirt of her green silk dress, smoothing it out over the posh limo seats. "Connor is fine. And he seems to be enjoying himself."

R.J.'s laughter was brusque. "I'm sure he is."

"Don't be snide, R.J."

He didn't answer, choosing instead to take a swallow of champagne.

Megan sighed. "You'll feel better about Connor when you see him again at Thanksgiving dinner." She turned to Dana. "Of course, you'll be there now, too. We're going to love having you in the family."

Dana gave her a wan smile. And just how long would she be in the family? a tiny voice asked her.

THE RINGING PHONE disturbed Janelle from her day-dreams of wealth. A large home, a new car, vacations to the tropics—all the things that should have rightfully been hers since birth.

She pushed her hair away from her face and reached out with her left hand to snag the receiver. "Yeah?"

"What's up, sweetheart?"

Janelle bolted upright in bed, shoving aside the brochures spread out around her. "Petey?"

"That's 'Connor' to you, babe."

"Don't joke!" Janelle scooted to sit on the edge of the mattress, her heart racing. "It's all going well?"

"Like a dream. You wouldn't believe how easy it's been. The condo she set me up in is posh. I could get used to this."

"I'm worried, Petey."

His sigh was long and aggrieved. "All right. What is it now?"

Janelle rolled her eyes. The man could be so obtuse. "There's still been no sign of Lacy?"

"Nope. No word of any dead women being found."

"Damn."

"Relax, babe. I told you, it's not that big of a deal these days. Dead bodies turn up all the time." His chuckle grated along her nerves. "Besides, the Maitlands have had other things to occupy them, like the living, breathing bodies. You wouldn't believe all the ruckus over the baby. Every single male Maitland around is being accused of dumping that kid. They're all running in circles—it's pretty damn funny."

Janelle clutched the worn chenille spread with her free hand. "Well, don't you dare act amused, Petey, do you hear me? You be humble and gracious and sincere." Why did she have to tell him how important this was? "When you all get together for Thanksgiving, make them believe the only thing you want is family. Once I claim the baby and explain our 'dire' situation, they'll get sucked in and we'll be on easy street!"

"I'm a born actor, sweetheart. I told the old lady how shocked I was to find out Clarise wasn't my real mother, that I'd been stolen from my rightful mother at birth, and she just ate it up. I told her I didn't want to cause her trouble, I just wanted to know her, since she was my ma." He laughed. "She's been real motherly ever since."

"What about the baby? Does anyone suspect anything?"

"With me? Nah. Not since I've told them it couldn't be mine."

"Still, Petey, keep on the lookout for any news about Lacy. Any bodies found with a head wound—hell, any bodies at all—I want to know about it. I can't quit worrying until I know she's been located. A dead woman in the alley that close to the clinic would make front-page news, regardless of what else is going on!"

"Stop fretting. I'll let you know the second I hear anything."

As she hung up, a cloud of misgivings loomed over Janelle's head. The color brochure of a luxurious Hawaiian vacation resort was crumpled in her fist. She threw the wad of paper across the room.

Damn it, she had as much right to the Maitland fortune as any of them. Just because her father had turned out to be the black sheep didn't mean she should be denied her fair share. R.J. and Anna were his kids, too, and they were being pampered, so why shouldn't she? But until that damned Lacy was found, she wouldn't be able to rest easy.

Things would work out in the end, she swore silently. She and Petey would have the money, and they'd take the kid for protection. They'd live the good life—she'd make damn sure they did.

CHAPTER SIX

IT WAS SEVERAL HOURS later before the limo dropped Dana and R.J. off in front of his house. Dana had never been here before, and he wondered what she'd think of it.

Actually, he'd been wondering what she was thinking all day. She'd been totally closed off from him, playing the role of new bride to perfection while hiding any real emotion.

He didn't like it.

He liked his reactions to her even less.

Sitting in the limo, he'd taken special note of the way she crossed her legs—long legs, he had only recently realized. As she looked out the window, avoiding his eyes, he'd seen the way her chest rose and fell with nervous breaths and couldn't keep himself from imagining her naked.

Dana.

Somehow, the fact that he felt as if he'd known her forever, that she'd always been a friend, made the moment highly erotic. He'd bedded more than his fair share of beautiful women. Hell, even if he didn't have a healthy sex drive, he'd have been highly experienced.

Women chased him down, drawn by his money, his power, his connections. Several times the papers had labeled him Austin's most eligible bachelor—a title he'd intended to maintain forever.

Yet here he was married. *To Dana.*

She certainly hadn't come on to him for money, or for any of the other motives women had shown in the past. He'd offered her money and she'd refused. She staunchly insisted on keeping her independence, on supporting herself. She'd looked poleaxed when she discovered he'd bought her a ring, damn her, which had made him feel like an ogre. She should have known him better than that, and probably did, but she intended to stick to their agreement, which meant she expected nothing from him.

Except sex.

That fact had been eating away at his control all day. Playing the diligent bridegroom, touching her, kissing her, had added to his strain. Dana hadn't noticed, but he'd been half-hard since the judge had proclaimed them man and wife.

He needed to get the upper hand again, and he might as well start right now.

"Dana?"

She glanced at him as if she'd forgotten he was there. "Yes?"

The chauffeur was pulling the limo around the curving drive to the front door. Lazily, R.J. leaned back in his seat and looked her over. "I had my housekeeper prepare your room for you. She's put away all your clothes and the things that you sent over earlier. Anything else you need we can get later."

"All right."

She was too agreeable, and he didn't like it. "It's not very late yet, but all things considered, I thought you could take a brief tour of the house to familiarize yourself, then change into something more comfortable. We can have a drink out on the veranda and relax…before going to bed."

He saw her slender, pale throat move as she swallowed, and he congratulated himself for taking her off guard. God knew, she'd kept him off guard since making her tantalizing demand. His head still reeled whenever he thought of it.

As she turned to look at him directly, he noticed that her green eyes were brighter than the emeralds she now wore. "I thought we agreed we'd share a room."

Persistent witch. He kept his expression impassive and shrugged. "Our rooms connect, both by an inside door and the veranda. You'll be free to come and go as you please. I thought you might appreciate the privacy for dressing and bathing and doing your hair and—" he gestured with his hand. "—whatever else it is women do on a daily basis."

She nodded, again looking away from him.

He didn't like her lack of attention, and gently, deliberately, added, "You don't have to worry, Dana. I'll be available to you when you want my end of the bargain met."

Her gaze snapped back to his, and a rosy blush spread from her throat up. Intrigued, R.J. sat forward, keeping his eyes locked on hers, and slowly reached out to touch the emerald necklace with one finger. "Ah. Warmth. I did wonder if your blush was as hot as it appeared." His finger stroked beneath the small stone, then all around it. He smiled, and a slight tension invaded his muscles. "Even the gold is heated," he murmured.

Dana's breathing accelerated, but it was nothing compared with his own reaction. He enjoyed touching her, seeing her respond so freely. Her eyes drifted shut, and he looked at her pale skin where his rough finger slowly glided, going lower and lower.

As usual, her blouse was fully buttoned, but this one had something of a modestly scooped neckline. He wondered whether she'd chosen it to show off the emerald or to attempt to seduce him. He almost chuckled. Dana was reserved enough to think a small glimpse of collarbone might be enticing.

Strangely enough, she was right.

The limo stopped and the driver got out. R.J. straightened back in his seat and watched Dana struggle to regain her composure. She was still breathing a little roughly, still fidgeting when the door opened and the driver offered an arm.

With a mumbled thank you she got out of the car, then turned to stone as she surveyed his house. R.J.

watched her from the corner of his eye as he dispatched the driver. She looked positively stunned, taking in everything around her as if in disbelief. It was fairly dark, but he had installed lighting along the path and at key points around the grounds to draw focus to a particular plant or tree. The lights gave off a soft, muted yellow glow.

Stepping up behind her, R.J. put both hands on her shoulders and whispered near her ear, "What do you think of your new home?"

"Oh, it's beautiful!" But she wasn't looking at the house, only the gardens.

"So it'll do?" he teased.

She stepped away to touch the feathery leaves of a young Chinese fan palm. R.J. had had several of them planted in staggered groups around the front of the property, to act as both a privacy fence and an ornamental border. There were also southern magnolia and crape myrtle trees, but it was November so they weren't blooming. He wondered what she'd think of his house in the spring when every tree and bush was fresh and new with budding life, ripe with color.

Except she wouldn't be here in the spring. By then, all the problems should be resolved, and he could resume his normal life.

A life without a wife.

"There are fruit trees in the back," he told her, "and several flower gardens. This isn't the best time of year to view the trees, but tomorrow I'll show them to you, if you like."

She turned to smile at him. "I'd love that. Thank you."

Taking her arm, he led her along the cobbled walk toward the front doors, pointing out some of his favorite plants. "I like things to take their own natural shape rather than be pruned into little squares or circles. Everything is bushier and softer that way. This is a Camellia japonica."

"It's beautiful. And so many flowers."

"The japonica has a very long season. And of course, those are hostas surrounding it. I prefer the halcyon for the bluish color. I just had them thinned out this fall, so they're not as full as usual. But it gives the day lilies more room to spread."

She stepped away onto another path lined with pansies of every color. "What's that tree?"

R.J. put his hands in the pockets of his slacks and followed along, enjoying her enthusiasm, the heavy darkness of the night. Her scent drifted back to him, noticeable even among all the fragrant flowers.

The evening was pleasant, around seventy degrees, with a bright moon and a multitude of stars. The lighting system gave the yard the look of early dusk, but it left deep shadows in Dana's bright green eyes. She looked... mysterious. "This one's a pink dogwood. The flowers are gone, of course, but the leaves turn such a brilliant scarlet in fall, as you can see, so it's always showy. One of my favorites."

She took off again, getting farther and farther from the house. "And that one?"

With a low, pleased chuckle, R.J. followed. Then he answered all her questions, which were numerous.

It was almost half an hour later when it dawned on him that Dana had effectively sidetracked him from his plans. Here it was his wedding night, and his new bride had him ambling around the grounds of his house looking at shrubs and trees and various types of mulch. Hell, they'd even discussed underground watering systems. He felt like an ass, and worse, he felt strangely vulnerable.

Damn her. He didn't like feeling out of control.

"Enough, Dana," he said when she started to question him on the homemade bench placed beneath a trellis of lush purple clematis. He managed, just barely, to keep the annoyance and inner turmoil out of his voice. "Don't you think it's time we went inside? I'd like to show you your room."

"Does my room have a view of the grounds?"

He caught her arm and started her back toward the path. Her French twist had begun to slip, and instead of being neatly anchored as usual, her hair looked softer and slightly tousled.

"Your room faces the back overlooking a fountain. There's a row or two of Sparkle berry, which you'll enjoy because they're loaded with bright red berries right now, and the birds flock to them."

She stepped away from him to turn a full circle, her arms outstretched, her face tilted to the endless sky above. "This is like a fairy-tale castle, R.J.," she said in a breathless whisper, "with so many gorgeous plants and colors and scents. I feel like I could get lost out here. I had no idea you knew so much about gardening."

That wasn't much of a surprise, since no one, other than his housekeeper, knew about his fascination with plants and his affinity for digging in the dirt. And he preferred to keep it that way.

Why in hell he'd opened up so completely to Dana, he couldn't guess.

She continued to stare into the star-studded sky, oblivious to his turmoil. If she'd been aware of it, he thought with a wry smile, he had no doubt she'd try to find a way to fix it for him.

For some reason, that thought perturbed him. She looked so happy and carefree, her fair hair glowing in the combined moon and lamp light, a few tendrils ruffled by the soft breeze, and suddenly he was restless, overcome by a vague longing. It was a wholly uncomfortable feeling, and he scowled. Snatching her hand as she twirled past once again, he pulled her against his chest and leaned down until their mouths were only separated by a breath.

"This is very private land, Dana. I know you haven't bothered looking at the house, but I chose it for its isolation. If you'd like, we could have our wedding night right here, beneath the weeping willow with the begonias all around us. Would you like that?"

Her eyes widened, looking dark and deep in the dim light, and her mouth fell open. He took advantage of the moment to kiss her, knowing it would distract her and embarrass her and most likely excite her. He felt as if he could deal with any one of those emotions far easier than he could the naked happiness he'd read in her expression.

It was the first time he'd ever seen her look that way, and the look was incredibly potent.

She was stiff in his arms for about three seconds, then her hands slid up his shoulders to his head and she gripped his hair hard as a groan escaped her, her mouth moving against his, her body pushing into his. She nearly pulled his hair out as she tried to get closer. She accepted his tongue, then went one further and sucked on it. R.J. gasped, her passion both astounding and seductive. He caught her wrists and gently eased her hands away before she could do more damage to his scalp.

"Easy, sweetheart. I like my head where it is."

She either didn't hear or didn't understand his teasing comment. Pressed full against him, she went on tiptoe and tried to find his mouth again. R.J. leaned back, laughing softly to himself. She was such a sweet surprise! As long as she was amusing him, there'd be no problem.

He cupped her face between his hands to gain her attention, then asked, "Is that a yes? Do you want to strip for me now and lie down on the soft grass? The air is a little fresh, but I think we'll manage to stay warm enough once we get things started."

Very slowly, awareness seeped back into her soft eyes. Her brows rose and her pupils flared. She scrambled out of his reach, crossing her arms over her chest in an oddly protective gesture that made him want to hold her again, gently this time, to comfort her.

"No." She shook her head, and her hair threatened to come completely undone. One long tendril dropped down across her forehead, fascinating him and making her huff with impatience. "I have no intention of… of…"

He wanted badly to smooth her hair and started to do just that. "Frolicking among nature?" He knew he was obsessed with her hair, like a pioneer male waiting anxiously to get a glimpse of a woman's ankle. Good God, it was only hair, and all women had it. It was just that Dana had always kept hers neatly pinned up, making his curiosity run wild.

She smacked his hand away before he could actually touch her. "It isn't funny, R.J.!"

Neither was his throbbing erection, but he was dealing with it the best he could. Which was evidently far better than she could deal with her own arousal. Dana had a tendency to get snippy when she was turned on or sexually frustrated. He'd found that out each time he kissed her. He wondered what would happen when she could let all that passion loose, rather than struggle to restrain it.

He wondered what would happen tonight.

Smiling, he looped his arm around her shoulders and again tried to get her on the winding path that led to the front door. "No doubt Betty, my housekeeper, heard the limo and is waiting for us. She'll have no idea what we're doing out here."

"That's a relief!"

R.J. was feeling just contrary enough to give her a squeeze. "We're married now, sweetheart. We can damn well cavort wherever we please." And soon, he'd be cavorting with her in *her* bed, where he intended to leave her. He liked his privacy, whether she valued her own or not. He expected to consummate the marriage with as little fuss as possible, pleasing her, pleasing himself, but no more than that. He'd remain detached and efficient and he'd fulfill her demands while still keeping as much emotional distance from her as possible. It could be done; he'd had sex with any number of women without feeling a single thing beyond physical satisfaction.

And afterward he'd hold her until she dozed off, then retreat to his own room.

He liked sleeping alone, damn it, and he expected to go on liking it. He was thirty-nine years old and he'd never before been inclined to share his bed. He didn't intend to start now.

If she wanted to repeat the procedure nightly, well,

who was he to complain about an available lover? He'd always had a very healthy sex drive, and no doubt the arrangement would prove convenient.

She'd be happy with the bargain, damn her, and he'd still keep himself safe.

Betty was waiting at the door when they reached it, her large brown eyes curious, her hands clutched together at her rounded middle. She was more than twenty years his senior, but as spry as a teenager and as protective and bossy as a surrogate mother. When they neared, a wide smile broke out over her pleasant face.

"There you are! I wondered what happened to you."

"Sorry if we worried you, Betty." R.J. pressed Dana forward. "My bride showed an unexpected interest in the grounds."

Dana reached a hand out. "Hello, Betty. I'm Dana Dillinger."

R.J. made a tsking sound. "How soon they forget. It's Dana Maitland now, love. At least, if that's what you want."

"Oh." Dana looked almost bewildered as Betty took her hand in a warm welcome.

The housekeeper, who thought any outdoor activity was thoroughly heinous, gave Dana an inquiring look. "The grounds?"

"All the beautiful trees and shrubs," Dana clarified.

"Oh, yes. Mr. Maitland does like puttering around outside." Her nose had wrinkled slightly, and then she ushered them both inside. "Come on in, now. I have everything ready for you."

To R.J.'s surprise, Dana didn't show nearly as much interest in the interior of the house as she had the gardens. Not that his home was a design showpiece. It was a modest two-story, situated in a quiet location. He was only one man and had no need for a much larger place. When he'd chosen the house, which had been built at the turn of the century, but recently renovated, it had been for the privacy, the abundance of land and the architectural charm. He loved the arched doorways and wooden floors and trim, the wide back veranda and original windows. The place had been professionally decorated, and many of his furnishings were antique, in keeping with the age of the house.

Dana gave a cursory glance at the entrance hall, peeked into the dining room at the right and the living room at the left, then peered at the curving staircase.

Betty started in that direction, leading the way up the stairs. "Your bags arrived earlier, and I've already put everything away." When they reached the top, she turned to the right to a pair of connecting bedrooms with private baths. To the left were two guest bedrooms and a hall bath.

"The kitchen is downstairs, just beyond the dining room," Betty explained, "and at the back of the house is a den with a nice library, and a workout room that's adjacent to an enclosed porch with a hot tub."

She turned and smiled at them both. "Dana, your

bathroom is right through that door. I put all your toiletries away so you shouldn't have any trouble finding what you need. Here's the closet, and I've already arranged all your things." The door leading to R.J.'s room stood open.

He saw Dana bite her lip and knew she felt uncomfortable that Betty knew of the sleeping arrangements. He gave his housekeeper a hug and said easily, "Thanks, Betty, for staying late and for getting everything organized so well."

She sent a stern look his way. "It's not every day you get married, Mr. M., now is it? I was glad to stay and help out. Besides, I had to meet your bride! Having a woman in the house is going to be quite a change."

"You're a sweetheart. But we can manage from here, so you might as well head home. And, Betty, take the day off tomorrow, all right?"

She winked at Dana. "I was planning to! I've already put a casserole in the refrigerator, and there's salad makings and a fresh-baked pie for dessert. The refrigerator is stocked with plenty of things for lunch, and I made sure no one else was set to come to work tomorrow." In an aside to Dana, she explained, "Mr. M. has a regular man to mow the lawn and another to tend the pool and the hot tub. All things considered, I figured that could be put off for a couple of days."

"Remind me to give you a bonus, Betty."

"Ha! I'll hold you to that." She squeezed Dana's hand

again then bustled out the door, saying over her shoulder, "I'll lock up on my way out."

Betty was no sooner gone and the bedroom door closed softly behind her than Dana began to fidget. R.J. gave in to a private, very indulgent smile of satisfaction. Naturally she was nervous about being with him the first time, and that suited him just fine. He watched her walk to the window to look out into the garden below.

"How do you like your room?"

She jumped slightly at his voice, then glanced at him quickly over her shoulder. "It's lovely." She barely looked at the room, all her attention focused on the scene outside her window. "Who did it belong to before me?"

Ah. Was that a tinge of jealousy he heard? But that didn't make any sense, and in any case, he didn't want her to be possessive enough to feel jealousy. He decided it was no more than Dana's practical search for info. She always asked questions.

Slowly, R.J. approached her until he stood just a few inches behind her. He looked over her shoulder at the lighted fountain and flowers below, but he didn't touch her. Not yet. Let the tension build, he thought, knowing it would make things go that much smoother, and easier, when they got around to consummating their bogus marriage—as per her request. She wouldn't have the wit, or the interest, in insisting he stay the night with her, not when she was totally replete.

"This room was utilitarian. I had old files in here, a

comfortable chair where I could read. Because of the other two guest rooms, I never felt I needed another. People don't visit me overnight all that often."

Dana stiffened somewhat, turning her head just enough that he could see her profile. R.J. touched the tip of her nose. "No, Dana, not even women. A woman who wakes in your house in the morning likes to assume things that don't exist."

Still slightly turned away from him, she asked incredulously, "You're telling me no woman has spent the night with you here?"

"That surprises you? You've seen how easily the media can turn against you, even though I've always been very discreet. Can you imagine how it would've been if I'd advertised my personal affairs?"

She waited a moment, then nodded, as if accepting the truth of his words. "Who decorated the room? You?"

That made him laugh. "Hardly. I have a knack for landscaping, and I know what type of furniture I like, but when it comes to matching flowered spreads with pastel curtains…."

She stepped away from the window. For the first time she really observed the room, and judging by the look on her face, it was only then that she realized the room had been done specifically with a woman's tastes in mind.

The carpet was a soft cream, as were the walls, which featured stark white moldings at the ceiling and floor.

The furniture was light oak with a natural sheen, new, yet crafted with the care and detail of days gone by. The spread on the queen-size bed was a bright splash of pastel flowers with an abundance of velvety throw pillows in every shape and color. Feminine, but not overly so.

The dust ruffle was edged with crocheted lace. Fresh flowers were arranged in vases around the room, and the lightweight curtains had been drawn back to allow in the moonlight and the muted glow from the gardens.

R.J. spoke softly, watching the expressions flickering across her face. "I sort of judged what I wanted by looking at Anna's rooms. I hope you approve. I hired a designer, but specifically told her to style it for a woman with understated tastes and without a lot of fussiness."

Dana turned to gape at him. "Oh, my God! Your sister. Anna wasn't at the wedding."

R.J. turned to stone. "No, I didn't want Anna involved." His sister was very precious to him. Ever since they'd been dropped off at Megan and William's home when he had been only three and Anna little more than an infant, R.J. had been determined to protect her. That meant keeping her out of his lies and out of the public spotlight. He hadn't known for certain if the press would end up hounding them at the wedding, but it had been likely, and he'd wanted Anna as far from him as possible. He also hadn't wanted his sister to probe too closely into his reasons for his hasty marriage.

"R.J., she'll be hurt."

"Not after I explain." He wouldn't give Anna the full truth, but he would make her understand that he'd only been trying to protect her and his ten-year-old nephew, Will, from the relentless press. The thought of Anna's face ending up in some rag mag, as his own had been, filled him with a killing rage. He wouldn't let that happen.

Dana was watching him with a keen intensity, and he instinctively withdrew, concealing his thoughts instantly. He gave her a vague smile and kept his tone light. "I gather the room doesn't impress you."

"I like it very much."

She sounded far from sincere. "Honey, you live here now. You can feel free to change anything. I want you to be comfortable."

"The view is spectacular. Did I see a pond?"

His mouth quirked at her continued interest in the grounds. "Yes, filled with fat goldfish. I put it in over the summer. I'm surprised you could see it this time of night." The pond was a discreet distance from the house and was surrounded by lilies. It featured a small waterfall, as well as a few aquatic denizens, like the goldfish, frogs and some bottom feeders.

"Water is very reflective in moonlight."

More than ready to change the subject, he stepped forward and fingered a loose tendril of her hair. "So is your hair." He searched her face and found a touch of hesitancy, a little shyness and a dose of obvious eagerness. He grinned. "I think I'll go take a quick shower.

I'll join you here in about thirty minutes?" That should give her plenty of time to prepare herself. He had a vague image in his mind of Dana with her hair falling free, a sexy negligee draped over her body and a smile of welcome on her face.

His hands shook.

"That's...that's fine."

R.J. touched her cheek once again, gave her a quick peck, then formed a strategic retreat before Dana could realize just how badly he wanted her.

She could never know the effect she had on him.

He didn't even like to admit it to himself.

CHAPTER SEVEN

R.J. WAITED thirty-eight minutes exactly, not wanting to seem too anxious. But the truth was, his body had been invaded by a fine trembling that wouldn't abate. He felt rock hard from his nape down to his toes, all his muscles tense, his movements awkward, his heart beating much too fast.

Never had he needed a woman this badly, but then, never had there been so much plotting involved. If he wanted a woman, he made an advance. She either accepted it or not, and the outcome had never been very important to him. He hadn't become the most eligible bachelor in Austin without being aware of the perks involved. If one woman refused him, he could always find another.

Somehow, Dana was different.

Wearing only a pair of slacks, he gave a quick tap at the door between their rooms, then quietly opened it. After her insistence that they see this through, he half expected to find Dana in the bed, provocatively posed, waiting for him. He half expected a shimmer of moonlight to drift over her partially clad body, highlighting some seductive detail of a sexy negligee that displayed more than it covered.

He did not expect to find her standing in front of the damn window once again, looking outside. Her hair was down now, but neatly braided, the pale rope falling just below her shoulder blades. She glanced at him over her shoulder, her face shiny clean in the moonlight, her eyes wide.

She wore a long white, granny gown.

It should have been the most sexless thing he'd ever encountered, given that it covered her from throat to toes. Even the sleeves were long, fitting to her wrists. It had no detailing that he could discern, just yards and yards of material that hid her body from him completely.

And made him pulse with need.

God, she looked so innocent and sweet. Never in his life had he seen a woman wear such a garment. The sheer novelty of it was proving to be extremely erotic.

Without looking away from her, he closed the door behind him. He hadn't meant to do that, wanting the return to his own room to be as inconspicuous as possible. But he'd needed something to do besides gawk, so he'd closed the damn door.

"Dana."

She turned completely to face him, her hands laced together in front of her, eyes glowing. She'd turned off all the lamps, but with the curtains wide open there was enough moonlight flooding over her for him to see. Not the small details, but her form and the bed, everything that was necessary.

"I'm a little nervous," she whispered.

He drew a slow breath that didn't do a damn thing to calm his galloping heart and forced the necessary words through his constricted throat. "You can still change your mind, you know."

She shook her head in immediate denial, causing the braid to swing over her shoulder, where it landed softly against her breast.

"All right." He reached out his hand. "Then come here."

She moved away from the window—and the moonlight—which left her body only a vague shadow. Taking tentative steps, she crossed the room until she stood before him. R.J. didn't dare touch her anywhere but her hand, which she offered to him shyly. Her fingers were cold and taken by a slight trembling that couldn't be feigned.

"You braided your hair."

"It tangles easily."

Amusement nudged at his lust-fogged brain. "Honey, most women would have left it loose, anyway. It's sexier that way."

He sensed more than saw her slight shrug. "For some women, maybe. I don't…don't do *sexy* very well. And my hair…it's just straight. And fine. It's not very sexy hair, believe me."

He swallowed hard, barely absorbing the meaning

of her words. "I think I'd like to find out for myself, if you don't mind."

"You want me to unbraid it?" Her tone indicated that the prospect held little appeal for her.

He wanted her naked, spread out on the bed. He wanted to be inside her already. His muscles strained with the effort to reign in his urgency. *Absurd.*

"I'd like that very much." He'd have offered to do the deed himself, but he didn't think he could and still maintain control.

Dana released his hand and reached for the end of the braid. A cloth-covered band pulled free, and she placed it on the dressing table in a small dish. Her movements were only faintly visible in the dark room, a whisper of sound, a shifting shadow. Only her white gown, the glimmer of her wide eyes and her fair hair shone clearly, allowing him to track her movements.

With nimble fingers, she loosened the braid, separating each long tress until her hair was shining and free and he had to catch his breath. Not sexy? Who the hell had ever told her such a ridiculous thing?

Bent on seduction—hers, not his—he gathered a handful of her hair and caressed it. It was baby fine, just as she'd claimed, and very, very soft. It slipped through his fingers like warm water, and he wished very badly that he could see her better.

He imagined that hair trailing over his chest, his abdomen, his upper thighs. He barely bit back a groan, even as he trembled uncontrollably.

"You're wrong," he rasped.

She remained silent, and her wide eyes shone up at him in a sort of dazed confusion.

A gentle smile tugged at his mouth, despite his arousal. "Your hair," he explained in a gruff whisper. "It is sexy. Warm, silky. I can't believe you keep it put up all the time."

He could feel her restlessness before she asked, "Even...even if what you said were true, why would I wear it down?"

R.J. stared at her as the words sank in like a dose of reality. Why *should* she wear her hair down? Dana had never been a woman who tried to attract men. She didn't flirt, didn't pose, didn't indulge in casual banter. She was always perfectly attired and proper, her appearance neat and orderly, meant to draw male appreciation. She didn't wear clothing that accentuated any part of her femininity. If anything, her business suits tended to conceal.

The professional image she presented to the world pleased him immensely, both in her role as his executive secretary and as his friend and confidante. He didn't want anything to change, certainly not Dana. He didn't want to alter their relationship when it already felt so right.

He had to remember that. The last thing he wanted to do was convince her to change her look; he sure as hell didn't want any other man discovering how attractive she could be. She could keep her hair up, and it would suit him just fine.

He took her hand again and led her toward the bed, stopping right beside it. There was no moonlight here, just deep shadows and Dana's evocative scent. Taking her face in his hands, he bent low and whispered, "I suppose we should get things moving."

She stiffened at his words, as he'd known she would. But he needed to remind her—and himself—that this was part of their deal, not a love affair, regardless of how his voice shook when he spoke, or the way his hands trembled. They had a business arrangement, and he didn't want her to read any more into it than that.

First he kissed her cheek, then the very corner of her lips, before closing his mouth over hers. Despite her frozen posture, her lips opened softly beneath his. His heart drummed madly, confounding him and renewing his determination. Without preamble, he sank his tongue inside, then groaned aloud at the delicious taste of her. Her hands found his wrists and curled around them; her breathing deepened.

"Damn." He couldn't believe this was *his* Dana, his proper, restrained secretary who remained unflappable at even the most harried meeting, who faced disgruntled clients or upset contributors with cool poise and calm deliberation. The woman who'd confronted his temper many times without a single flinch.

Right now, she was simply a woman, shivering with need, low sounds of pleasure escaping her while he kissed her throat, her temple, her ear. He couldn't seem to make himself stop. He wanted, quite simply, to kiss her everywhere, to explore all the subtle fragrances and tastes of her body.

Yet she was still the same woman he'd always known but never regarded as a sexual being; his secretary, his friend, his Dana. *His wife.*

She pressed against him, trying to complete the contact of their bodies. Despite his resolve, it amazed and excited him that she had always looked so innocent. For all the time he'd known her, she'd seemed disinterested in sex, yet here she was, wriggling against him like a wanton woman.

He lifted one hand to close over her breast. R.J. was experienced in reading women, in picking up their nuances, knowing what pleasured them and when they wanted that pleasure. It was an awareness that made him a good lover. Dana wanted, needed to be touched, so he touched her.

Pure sensation shot through him at the feel of her. Her breast was soft and heavy beneath the fabric of her gown, and her small nipple tightened against his palm. He rubbed it with his open hand and she clutched at him, appearing both strangely bewildered and wildly excited. He heard her breath catch, felt her body shiver.

Kissing her voraciously, he forced her head to bend back to give him better access. The urge to tumble her onto the bed swamped him. He was so hard he hurt.

He pulled his mouth free to drag in a needed breath

of air, his body awash in heat. Dana left her head tipped back, her eyes closed, as she gave herself up to his touch.

It was too much.

He hooked his free arm beneath her buttocks and lifted her against his pelvis, pressing her into him until her soft thighs parted and he could stroke the soft notch of her thighs with his pulsing arousal.

She cried out, her hands again clutching at his hair, trying to bring his mouth back to hers.

Instead, he raised her a bit higher and drew her cloth-covered nipple into his mouth. She went wild.

Her movements weren't smooth or practiced, and they fired his lust. Her legs closed around his hips, and he took two quick steps forward until her back came up against the wall. He pinned her there with his body, nearly beyond rational thought.

The damned floor-length nightgown was in his way, and he struggled briefly with it, jerking it above her knees and then sinking his fingers into her soft outer thigh just below her buttocks.

"R.J.!"

She wasn't wearing panties. His palm encountered the firm contours of her bottom, and he groaned again, caught up in a fog of raging lust. It had never been like this for him, but then he'd never made love with a woman like Dana before, a feminine paradox, subtle one moment, fiercely blatant the next.

He wanted her naked, but he didn't know if he could

wait that long. He adjusted his hold, bringing his hand around the front to her smooth, silky belly. She stiffened the tiniest bit, her breathing suspended as his fingers stroked down and into her soft curls.

She jerked, but he held her tight, limiting her instinctive movements. He insinuated one finger between her delicate folds and touched her, overwhelmed by her heat, her wetness. "Oh, yeah." He squeezed his eyes shut. *"Hell, yes."*

His fingers stroked deeper, slowly, and she bucked against him, her breathing choppy, her fingers biting into his shoulders. "You want this, don't you, Dana? You're so damn hot." He pushed one finger into her and was amazed at the incredible tightness, the way her muscles spasmed, gripping his finger hard.

"R.J.?"

She'd gone still, but he wrote it off as expectant anticipation. If she was half as aroused as he was, he could understand her inability to move. He felt clumsy in his urgency to become part of her. He forced another finger deep and swallowed her groan with a long, devouring kiss.

There was a buzzing in his ears, a red haze blotting out the shadows in the room. Unable to wait a second more, he turned and lowered Dana to the mattress. Her legs hung over the side and she started to sit up, but he came down over her, between her widespread thighs. He kissed her quiet, until her arms were wrapped around his neck and her thighs moved restlessly alongside his.

"Don't move," he muttered, then levered himself up enough to shove the gown above her breasts. He couldn't see her in the darkness, and it frustrated him, but he was too close to the edge to start fumbling with the lights. He unzipped his pants and stripped them off, then hurriedly slid on a condom. The shaking in his hands enraged him, but thankfully it was too dark for her to see.

The welcoming softness of her body greeted him as he lowered his weight onto her. He almost growled at the exquisite sensation. In the back of his mind, he kept thinking, *Is this really Dana?* The reality of being with her like this was almost more than he could take. He'd always seen Dana as sexless, female efficiency in a suit. But the heat of her exposed body, the frantic beating of her heart and the soft cushion of her breasts beneath his chest proved she was very capable of indulging in even the most heated encounters. He'd been duped by her—and now he was learning the sweet truth.

Carefully he parted her with his fingers, struggling to go slowly, despite the urgency surging through him. He guided himself just inside, grinding his teeth at her heat, at her wetness as she closed around the very tip of him. Dana didn't move, didn't even breathe. He pressed forward with an effort, going a little deeper. She felt snug, unbearably so, tight enough to completely shatter his control.

With a rough curse he wrapped one arm around her trim hips, lifted her high and drove into her. He was met with natural resistance for a split second before her body opened to his and he sank deep with a raw groan of indescribable pleasure.

He had a single moment to absorb the pleasure of having his length wrapped tightly in moist heat, then Dana arched so violently she almost bucked him off. Her soft, nearly breathless gasp rang in his ears, and he realized several things at once.

Dana was no longer holding him tight. Her hands were pressed hard against his chest in an effort to shove him away. He didn't move.

Her breaths came in short, harsh pants, as if she were experiencing discomfort. Or worse. And he knew why.

She'd been a virgin.

Never in his life had he felt a woman so acutely. He'd been sexually active since his mid teens, but the tightness he felt now, squeezing him, nearly turning his mind to mush, was unique. He strained to hold himself perfectly still while his mind tried to assimilate all the facts. Her shallow, rapid breaths fanned his throat. Her small hands were hot against his chest. Her soft thighs encased his hips. And her body held him as if she'd never let him go.

"Dana?"

Several seconds passed in silence. He heard her swallow. "I…I'm sorry."

He couldn't begin to understand what she was apologizing for. "You're a virgin?"

She moved, shifting beneath him, and instinctively

he used his hips to pin her down again, grinding into her softness in reaction.

"R.J...." She moved again, lifting her legs so that her feet pressed flat against the mattress.

The position brought him deeper still, and his gut tightened painfully. He didn't know if she was trying to escape him or seduce him. All he knew for certain was that he was so deep, and the pleasure so keen, he was ready to explode.

His arms wrapped snug around her, his face pressed into her neck, he thrust hard, two times, three. He growled like a savage, thoroughly shattered, drained of all rational thought, his body balanced on an edge of pleasure so keen he'd never known anything like it.

Afterward he couldn't seem to do more than breathe—and even that required strenuous effort. They were still hanging half over the bed, Dana's legs now limp beside his. When they started to slip to the floor, he hefted himself onto his back beside her with a groan.

Like a shot, Dana was off the bed.

R.J., trying to regain normal breathing, watched as she hustled into the bathroom, her white nightgown a bright beacon as she dashed across the dark room.

He wanted to call her back, but he remained silent, listening to water run in the bathroom, trying to imagine what she was thinking while his heartbeat gradually slowed and his brain cleared of the fog that had taken over rational thought.

She hadn't found a bit of pleasure.

No, that wasn't true. She'd been every bit as turned on as he before he'd lost control and more or less attacked her. Shame washed over him. Damn, he'd been like a rutting animal.

He squeezed his eyes shut and silently called himself ten times a fool. Hell, he'd wanted to explore her entire silken body, yet he'd spent less than ten minutes on that particular pleasure, and had touched her only in the ways necessary to have her, without all the tenderness and detail he knew women wanted and needed.

He'd wanted to taste her everywhere, yet he'd barely kissed her, and certainly not in the ways and places he'd intended. She'd discovered the start of pleasure, the tip of the iceberg, but not the explosive conclusion.

And once he'd gotten inside her, he'd lost all claim to control.

It had never happened to him before and made no sense. She was Dana, for God's sake, not some femme fatale who'd deliberately seduced him. She'd done no more than stand there in her prim gown with her hair braided like a schoolgirl's, and he'd been as aroused as if he'd been indulging in hours of foreplay.

Hell, even when he *had* indulged in hours of foreplay, he'd never been that turned on.

Dropping an arm over his eyes, he groaned. There was still a pleasant buzz in his body, a sexual repletion that echoed. His muscles felt like mush.

And his bride was in the bathroom, hiding, maybe crying.

He couldn't stand it. He forced himself to his feet and staggered to the closed door. "Dana?"

The water shut off. Silence throbbed in the dark bedroom.

"Dana?" he repeated.

"Yes?"

Her voice was too high, too light. Very forced. He moaned low in his throat, thoroughly disgusted with himself. He felt like a defiler of innocents, and he didn't like the feeling at all. He hadn't lost control like that... ever. Spreading one hand on the wall, he propped himself up, still unsure of his shaky legs. "Honey, are you all right?"

A short, twittering laugh. "Yes, yes, of course. I'm fine."

His free hand curled into a fist, and his eyes narrowed in speculation. He wanted to see her, to judge for himself. She'd been in the bathroom a long time. "What are you doing in there?"

"Oh, nothing. Tidying up."

Tidying up what? Was she torturing her hair back into that twist? Or braiding it again? Surely it didn't take this long.

Another thought occurred to him, making him scowl. Her body had been so incredibly tight, had he hurt her? Would she tell him if he had? The answer to that was a resounding no. In all the time he'd known her, he'd never heard Dana complain, so he knew damn good and well she wouldn't start now, and certainly not over this.

R.J. rubbed his face and leaned against the wall beside the door, waiting. He liked to think he would have been more gentle if he'd known she was a virgin, but he couldn't force himself into that lie. He'd known. Not right away, of course, but the second he'd gotten inside her, realization had walloped him with the force of a sledgehammer. It made sense in so many ways. She'd always been reserved, dedicated to work. He'd never heard a single rumor of her dating.

But she was nearly thirty years old, and very, very special; caring, comforting, intelligent. Surely some man somewhere had appreciated those qualities and given it his best shot?

R.J. shook his head in wonder, because he'd known her forever and he'd never even considered such a thing himself. He and Dana had a special relationship, and not once had he thought of risking that by introducing a sexual involvement. He could have sex with other women, but what he had with Dana couldn't be found anywhere else.

He turned his head and stared toward the closed bathroom door. Damn, but he'd blundered badly. The knowledge of being the first, the *only* one, obliterated everything else.

Sweat beaded on his forehead and he clutched the doorknob, rattling it once. He wasn't surprised to find it was locked. "Come on out, Dana. I want to talk to you."

Another lengthy silence, then finally, "I, uh, I'll be

out in a bit. Why don't you go on to bed? You've had a long day."

He'd had a long day?

"We can talk in the morning," she added, sounding desperate.

R.J. started to insist, then caught himself. At this moment she wasn't his secretary, and he wasn't her boss. She was his wife, and due some courtesy, belated as it might be.

He couldn't really blame her for not wanting to talk to him. And he wasn't at all certain that now was the best time, anyway. She wanted to be alone.

Hell, he had wanted to retreat to his room, had planned to do just that. He'd wanted to maintain his privacy and stay detached. Now she obviously wanted the same thing. Here was his opportunity, yet he felt oddly reluctant to leave her this way.

"Dana, I think we should—"

The water came back on, drowning out his words. He didn't feel like shouting to be heard, damn it. So he'd goofed? He could explain things to her in the morning. He'd convince her he was a good lover and promise he'd make certain she found her own satisfaction next time. He'd tell her that she'd taken him by complete and utter surprise.

And he'd make damn sure she explained a few things, as well. Like how the hell an attractive twenty-nine-year-old woman had remained a virgin.

They could both use a good night's sleep to regroup. Then they'd talk, just as she suggested.

R.J. turned away, but he was followed by a feeling of foreboding. He glanced at the bed as he passed it, noticing how a shaft of moonlight danced just beyond the reach of the mattress, spreading out over the floor.

He'd made love to Dana, but she hadn't enjoyed it. He'd touched her intimately, yet he hadn't seen so much as that glimpse of an ankle he'd imagined earlier.

He'd had sex with his wife, but he hadn't even had the courtesy to undress her. Her nightgown had been bunched up under her arms, and her breasts had remained covered.

His eyes squeezed shut in disgust and self-loathing. He'd taken his wife with all the finesse and consideration of a sailor on one-day shore leave.

But he had seen her hair loose, he reminded himself, and that alone was enough to keep him tossing and turning for the rest of the night.

CHAPTER EIGHT

DANA HAD NEVER been accused of being a coward, but she felt very cowardly at the moment. She wanted nothing more than to stay in her room and hide all day, yet she'd heard R.J. go downstairs some time ago. He'd be wondering where she was, thinking he'd cowed her with his detached, emotionless brand of sex.

What had she been thinking when she'd made that horrendous bargain? She wasn't a woman who could indulge in meaningless sex. Especially not when it was with a man she'd loved for so many years.

She sat at her dressing table and brushed her hair, then expertly twisted it up at the back of her head. A few pins, and she felt more like herself.

Except that she had a hickey on her neck.

She stared at the small mark with appalled fascination, remembering R.J.'s mouth there, the heat of it, the nip of his teeth. He'd made a low, guttural sound of intense satisfaction as he'd come inside her, his whole body rigid, shaking, hot. She shuddered and squeezed her eyes shut.

Dana Dillinger, plain Jane extraordinaire, had a

hickey from the most eligible bachelor in Austin, Texas!

She almost giggled. Then she remembered her name wasn't Dillinger anymore, and she groaned.

Her whole body bore signs of his lust—lust for *her*. Though they'd been covered by her nightgown, her breasts were tender from his hands and mouth and the press of his heavy chest after he'd climaxed. The insides of her thighs felt achy from the strain of opening wide for him, gripping him, and later, from trying to push away from him.

He hadn't hurt her, not really. In fact, for the most part she'd felt a pleasure beyond any she'd ever imagined. But the depth of his response had left her shaken.

Because it had only been physical for him.

Last night, all pretenses of the civilized business-man had vanished, replaced with ruthless determination and unrestrained desire. He'd shown no inhibitions, no reserve. She knew R.J. well enough to understand he could be that way, but she hadn't expected him to be that way with her.

And she knew she couldn't deal with it.

If he'd been suave and practiced and gentle, she could have held back her emotions and taken what he offered. But R.J. had been sensually intrusive, touching her in ways she hadn't been prepared for, ways that should have been about love, not just sex.

Knowing she'd had only part of him had left her feeling more alone than ever.

She shook her head at her fanciful, old-fashioned conclusions. No, it would be better if they went back to his original plan. Last night as she'd lain in her new bed, painfully aware of R.J. sleeping only a short distance away, she considered everything with new eyes. She loved R.J. enough to do anything in her power to help repair his reputation—anything except pretend she didn't love him while they were intimately joined. That was asking too much.

She couldn't feign an emotionless, loveless physical attraction that would allow them to sleep together. It simply wasn't in her.

And he hadn't even wanted her to. She'd been the one to insist.

Well, he'd be relieved when he found out she'd changed her mind.

Dressed in comfortable beige drawstring cotton slacks and a matching long-sleeved tunic, she left the seclusion of her room.

The house was eerily silent as she made her way downstairs. Surprisingly, the air conditioner wasn't on; instead, R.J. had opened all the windows. In mid-November, the air was cooler, refreshingly so, and she welcomed the breeze that lifted the curtains and filled the house with the scents of the flowers outdoors.

Hoping for coffee to clear the cobwebs, she found her way to the kitchen, glancing at the house as she went. It was cozy and well decorated, and it looked like R.J. If he'd had it done by an interior designer, she was certain he'd had a lot of input.

Smiling, she stepped into the kitchen—and stopped dead.

R.J. stood there sipping steaming coffee from a bright red mug. He was leaning against the counter next to the coffeemaker, ankles crossed, pose negligent.

He was wearing only a pair of well-worn jeans.

Her breath caught and held. Her heartbeat doubled.

R.J. looked up at her entrance, the coffee mug almost to his mouth, and his hazel eyes pinned her, gleaming with intent. "Good morning."

Though she didn't intend it to, her gaze moved over him. God, he was incredibly gorgeous, all hard bone and smooth muscle and visible strength. His dark hair was still damp from his shower, combed back from his forehead so that his angular face seemed more pronounced, more male than ever. His jaw was freshly shaved, and beneath the strong smell of coffee she could detect a spicy cologne. Her skin tingled with awareness.

He had one hand braced on the counter at his hip, and the other held the mug, which he used to salute her. Still she stared. His chest was broad, and she remembered feeling the crisp hair and hard muscle beneath her open palms last night. She wondered what it might have felt like on her naked breasts, tantalizing her nipples.

A rush of heat rose inside her and quickly spread outward until she knew she was blushing furiously.

R.J. chuckled. "Cat got your tongue this morning?"

She forced her gaze away from her fascinated study of his hard abdomen and reached for the empty mug he'd left sitting on the counter. The movement brought her close to him, and she did her best not to react to his scent, to his warmth, which she could feel enveloping her. "Good morning, R.J."

She turned her back to pour the coffee—a tactical error. R.J.'s mug clattered down beside her own, and his arms came around her from behind, his hands flattening on the counter, caging her in. She stiffened, the coffee carafe clutched tightly in her hand.

He nuzzled her nape. "Mmm. I've been waiting down here for you, hoping you weren't a slugabed."

"I…I never sleep late." Oh, my God, it felt so wonderful to have him kissing her neck that way, little kisses that were barely there, a soft brushing of his lips. It made her skin tingle and her insides curl. His thighs touched the backs of her own, teasing then moving away again. She caught her breath and held it.

He lifted his right hand from the counter and flattened it on her middle, making her gasp. His long, rough fingers moved idly. "I like what you're wearing. Do you realize I've never seen you out of a suit?"

"R.J.…."

"Last night," he whispered, his tone husky, "it was so dark, I could barely see you at all."

Thank God! She'd wanted it dark because she knew she wasn't the type of woman he was used to—sexy, self-assured, knowledgeable in how to please a man in bed.

His mouth paused, and he moved a slight distance away. He drew his hand from her stomach, which gave her the chance to breathe in a huge lungful of air, and then he reached up to the neckline of her tunic. He found the chain on the necklace he'd given her.

"You're wearing it."

She hadn't taken it off, not once. She didn't ever want to forget the moment he'd given it to her, so gallantly telling her it matched her eyes. Those were the sweetest, most romantic, most meaningful words she'd ever heard, and she'd cherish them always.

"Dana?"

"Shouldn't I wear it?" She'd kept the necklace hidden beneath her tunic, and the bracelet was concealed by the long sleeves. But suddenly she had the feeling she'd made a mistake. She knew so little about jewelry, and even less about gifts from men. "I mean, I know it's not exactly appropriate with casual clothes…"

"Dana, it's appropriate for you all the time. I told you, you look incredible in emeralds." His hands clasped her waist and he turned her to face him. Bending his knees slightly so he could look her straight in the eyes, he asked in a low voice, "Were you wearing it last night?" His eyes were bright, intent. His breath touched her lips as he spoke, and his fingers bit into her waist. "And the bracelet?"

He was so close, his eyes searching. His bare chest

beckoned her, and she wanted badly to touch him, to tangle her fingers in the dark hair, to search out his nipples. Her heartbeat raced and she swallowed hard. Trying desperately to control the aberrant urges, she kept her hands firmly at her sides and tightened them into fists. "Yes."

His pupils flared and he drew in a quick breath. His gaze lowered, and she knew he was looking at her breasts. She looked down, too, and was appalled to see her nipples were puckered tight, pressing against the soft fabric of the tunic, clearly visible even through her bra. Her gaze shot back up to R.J.'s, and she found him watching her with a calculating intensity.

He's trying to decide how to handle me, she thought. She'd seen him do it so many times in his business dealings, assessing the situation, planning his maneuver. She took several slow, calming breaths, sorting her thoughts. Probably he was as embarrassed about last night as she was, and searching for the gentlest way to handle things. Maybe he assumed the deal was still on. Just the thought made her shudder.

She should let him off the hook right now, before things got out of control.

R.J. tugged her slightly closer. "About last night…"

With a short laugh meant to hide her nervousness, Dana twisted away from him. "Last night was a mistake."

"What?"

"A total failure." The only place to go was to the

other side of the small kitchen table, so she did, moving behind a chair and holding on to the back of it. R.J. tracked her every movement with his eyes, as if waiting for her to bolt, or to attack. She realized that for once, he had no idea what she was doing or thinking.

He turned to the coffeepot and poured her a cup, then reached across the table to place it close to her. A tray with sugar and cream was already there, but she couldn't quite deal with it.

He retrieved his own cup and sipped, and she could tell by his expression he was carefully gauging his next words, judging them for effect. Once again he took up his casual pose. "I'll admit last night didn't go quite as I'd planned—"

"I take full blame."

Both of his brows shot up at her blurted interruption, as if she'd said the unexpected. He watched her a moment, but when she only chewed on her bottom lip, he asked, "You do?"

"Absolutely. It was my idea, after all."

That caused one side of his mouth to twitch, and she knew if he laughed at her she'd throw the coffee at his head. But of course he didn't laugh. He was more calculating than that.

"What I recall," he said, his gaze probing, "is that you were a virgin, so any planning beyond the very basics seems pretty far-fetched."

She hadn't been R. J. Maitland's secretary all this time without learning a tactic or two of her own. She had no intention of discussing her virginity with him—there was no way to explain it, anyway—so she skipped it entirely. To give herself something to do, she began dumping sugar in her coffee.

"R.J., I was the one who thought up the ridiculous plan of…sleeping together in the first place."

"Ridiculous?"

"Absolutely." She gave a resolute nod and stirred her coffee so quickly some sloshed out. She snatched up a napkin and dabbed at it. "I thought I might enjoy a casual…fling." She nearly choked and picked up her coffee to take a sip. It tasted like syrup! "But last night," she continued, looking him in the eye, "proved me wrong. I think we should go back to your original plan."

"My original plan?"

She frowned at him. It wasn't like R.J. to parrot words or stand there looking dumbstruck. The man generally had something to say on everything. "Yes. During the day, I'll be the best wife to you that I can be. I have several plans that might shore up your reputation—though I'm still not convinced it's necessary—and I'm more than ready and willing to implement them. But at night…"

"Lovemaking isn't limited to the evening, you know."

His harsh statement took her by surprise. He looked annoyed, maybe even bordering on anger. Why? She was offering him what he'd wanted all along. Heaven knew he'd fought hard enough for it before giving in.

"I beg your pardon?"

Very slowly, he rounded the table. "Married people have sex whenever they want, or are you too much the puritan to realize it?"

Her mouth opened, but nothing came out.

"In fact," he continued, coming closer still, "I'd intended to make love with you right here, right now, on the kitchen table."

"R.J.!"

"It's sturdy enough. That's not exactly why I chose the style in the first place, but as I was making the coffee, it occurred to me it was strong enough to support us, and it's just about the right height for all kinds of *interesting* things."

He was too close to her now, and she could see the dangerous glint in his hazel gaze. Curiously, she eyed the small table. It was heavy oak with a slab top. And... it did look sturdy.

"R.J., you're being ridiculous." But she felt flushed and anxious—and very hurt. She didn't want to be a mere body to him. She'd thought she could, but she'd been so wrong.

"Don't you want to know what those interesting things are, Dana?"

"No." *More interesting than what he'd already done?* She didn't think she could stand it.

"I want to tell you, anyway." He reached for her, and she ducked away.

"Well, I'd like that tour of the yard you promised. It's a beautiful day for it." She stopped and faced him when she was again on the opposite side of the table from him.

R.J. gave her a speculative glance, his long fingers rubbing his chin. She saw the exact moment he came up with a plan.

"All right, Dana. Why don't we get some breakfast together and eat out on the patio? I can show you all the plant specimens I've brought in."

Relief flooded her. "That'd be wonderful."

"I knew you'd think so."

Was he laughing at her? Had her relief been so obvious? She frowned as she asked, "What would you like for breakfast?"

"Are you offering to cook for me? Is that one of those wifely duties you don't mind fulfilling?"

She'd spoiled him, she decided. He felt free to bait her because she'd always allowed him to as her boss. She'd waited on him, been the best secretary she could, because she loved him and wanted to make herself indispensable to him. But if they were going to get along during the duration of their bogus marriage, there would need to be some new ground rules.

Explaining things to R.J. wouldn't work. He'd instinctively balk at having rules laid out for him. So instead she'd have to show him by example. She went to the refrigerator and opened the door. "I'll do breakfast," she said casually "but then you have to do lunch. There's fresh fruit in here, and bagels. We can have that for breakfast."

R.J. was again watching her when she pulled the cantaloupe and fat strawberries from the fridge. He eyed her loaded hands and nodded. "I can toast the bagels. Do you like cream cheese on yours?"

He stepped close, then reached past her into the refrigerator and retrieved the bagels and cream cheese. His arm brushed her breasts, and his broad chest was teasingly close. Dana held her breath, wanting to move away but unable to get her feet to cooperate.

As he started to step past her, he dropped a hard, quick smooch on her open mouth and grinned. Dana stared up him.

"Dana?"

"Hmm?"

"Cream cheese?"

As if coming out of a daze, she shook her head and glared at him. "Yes, please."

R.J. chuckled and sauntered away. He thought he had it all figured out, she knew. And she'd just made it embarrassingly easy for him. Well, no more. She wouldn't get that close to him again.

This evening she'd start a campaign for improving his public image. That ought to keep them both busy enough to forget about last night.

Or at least to pretend to forget.

"I'M SUPPOSEDLY an excellent lover, you know."

Dana choked on her melon, nearly spitting it out on the table. It took her several gasping breaths and two sips of tepid coffee to clear her throat.

Damn him, he'd taken her completely off guard.

They were out on the enclosed patio, the beautiful sunshine reaching in through the open windows, the hot tub bubbling warmly at the far end. Birds flew around the yard, providing entertainment, while the flowers within the room itself continually drew her attention. They'd spent the past hour chatting about those flowers, and a dozen other innocuous topics. She'd started to relax, to let down her guard. But then he'd made that outrageous comment.

R.J. didn't smile at her shocked reaction. He simply continued to watch her as she wiped her mouth with a napkin and glowered at him.

When she made no reply, he pressed her. "You *do* know that, don't you, Dana?"

He wasn't going to let it go, so she shrugged, pretending an indifference she was far from feeling. "I'll take your word for it."

His eyes narrowed the tiniest bit.

She decided she needed to change the subject again, and quickly.

"Shouldn't you be getting dressed, R.J.?" No sooner had she spoken the words than she inwardly groaned. She couldn't have picked a worse thing to comment on. But then, his half-naked body was all she could really focus on. She'd made appropriate enough responses as he'd enthused over his flowers, telling her which ones did best indoors, which needed shade and which needed sunlight.

And she truly was interested—but not when R.J. Maitland was within touching distance and wearing only a pair of faded worn jeans that fit his lean body like a second skin.

She wasn't used to such close proximity to any man; breakfast after a night together was an aberration. But for that man to be R.J. was enough to keep her totally flustered.

R.J. leaned back in his wrought-iron chair and stretched. "Why should I pile on the clothes? There's only me and my wife present. And it's a weekend. After suffering suits all week, I prefer to relax on the weekend." He leaned forward, and in a conspiratorial tone admitted, "I actually hate suits. I prefer jeans any day."

Trying to maintain her dignity, Dana smiled. "No one would ever know. You wear your suits well."

"As well as I wear my jeans?"

The thought of throwing the rest of her coffee at him appealed to her greatly. However, she considered herself above such childish acts. "Actually, the jeans suit you better."

He settled back in his chair and tilted his head, his gaze thoughtful. "How so?"

Dana shrugged. If he insisted on playing this game, she'd do her damnedest to match him. But then, it had

100

always been that way. R.J. would roar and stomp, and she simply kept pace with him. That was one of the reasons she had succeeded as his employee when others had failed. "You're a barbarian at heart, R.J. That much is obvious. The suits may hide it from some people, but not from me."

To her surprise, his mouth tightened. "Last night was no example of my character."

Her eyes widened. She hadn't been thinking of last night! Good grief, did he really think she'd deliberately bring it up? "As far as I'm concerned, last night is best forgotten."

That didn't appear to appease him at all, so she tried again. "I was referring to your controlling ways—at the office, with your family. You like to sit back and observe people, then force them to do your bidding without them even knowing it."

His face went blank with surprise. "What the hell are you talking about?"

"You think I haven't noticed?"

"I think you're damn well imagining things!"

"R.J." She made a tsking sound. "You do it all the time. You manipulate. Not in a mean-spirited way, because you're not a mean or petty man. You're just a man who likes things his own way. And you have very set ideas on what's best, for yourself and for everyone else. So you control things. You keep yourself apart from others so you can maintain that control."

His eyes were diamond hard, his jaw set. "I don't seem to have a hell of a lot of control over you."

"I have the advantage of being wise to your ways." A variety of expressions flickered through his hazel eyes, but mostly disgruntled resentment. He didn't like it that she had pegged him so neatly. Still, there was also a touch of admiration, and she basked in it. R.J. had told her many times that he greatly respected her intelligence. She'd valued the compliment each time he'd given it.

He chewed his upper lip a moment, deep in thought, then he smiled. It wasn't a smile to put her at ease. Just the opposite.

"So tell me, smarty-pants. If you're so attuned to me, what am I thinking right now?"

"Probably about some way to get the upper hand."

He slowly shook his head. "Wrong. But I'll tell you anyway."

She started to stand, using the excuse of carrying in their dishes. She didn't trust the iron determination in his voice and thought a strategic retreat was in order.

Before she could get completely out of her seat, though, he'd taken her arm and held her in place. "I'm thinking about how different you look in these clothes. Do you know I can see the shape of your behind? Well, almost. The top is too long and loose for me to get a good look, but it beats the hell out of those tailored suits you wear that reveal all the feminine curves of an army tank."

Appalled, Dana again tried to pull free. R.J. let her, but then stood to block her way. He wasn't being subtle in his domination, but then R.J. seldom used subtlety once he was set on his course. He walked his own path, and people generally got out of his way.

Dana stiffened her spine.

He stood very close to her, watching her intently, and she managed a smile, refusing to let him see how awkward she felt. "My behind is hardly worthy of all this discussion."

The tender touch of his hand on her cheek was shattering. "You forget," he whispered, "I may not have seen all of you last night, thanks to the darkness, but I sure as hell touched on all the important parts." He tipped up her chin, forcing her to meet his gaze. "I'm going crazy now wondering if you look as good as you feel. And let me tell you, your backside felt damn near perfect. Soft, round, just right for a man to hold on to."

If her face got any hotter she'd go up in a puff of smoke. "R.J.…." His name was spoken as a soft plea, barely heard—and R.J. answered by tilting his head and pressing his mouth to hers.

This isn't what you want, her mind screamed, but minds were easy things to ignore when the pleasure was so sharp. She'd been exceedingly preoccupied with R.J.'s chest and was now acutely aware of being pressed to it, of the steady, comforting thump of his heart, the silky-smooth hardness of his shoulders. Her hands crept over his biceps, thrilling at the thickness of iron muscle, before giving in and moving over his chest, exploring him as she'd so often thought of doing.

R.J. gave a deep groan of encouragement, his own hands idly coasting up and down her back, stopping just before cupping her bottom. Dana felt the crispness of his chest hair, the heat of his skin beneath. And the scents—R.J.'s scent was indescribably potent. She opened her mouth, wanting more of him, and his hot tongue slowly licked inside.

Oh…this was so different from last night. Now, with the sunshine bright in the cozy room, he could clearly see her. And though he didn't seem bothered by her unmistakable plainness, neither did he seem as carried away. He was moving too slowly, too…*methodically.*

Dana jerked away with a low gasp, knowing her eyes were round with distress. "We can't do this," she croaked.

He kept his arms around her, and she saw the fire in his eyes, the denial. "The hell we can't. We're married, remember?"

"No." She shook her head, and when she pushed against him, his arms fell to his sides. "You're doing it again—carefully figuring out how to get the upper hand. Doing whatever you need to do to keep it."

"That's what you think this is about?" His shoulder muscles were rigid, and his fierce frown carved deep grooves over his brow. "Control?"

His obvious anger didn't faze her. It never had. "Isn't it, R.J.?"

Moving too fast for her to avoid him, he snatched her wrist, holding her tightly but with careful restraint. His gaze locked on hers, he carried her hand to his groin and pressed it there. Beneath the denim she felt every masculine inch of him.

Her breath caught and held. Shock rushed through her, making her knees shaky, her chest tight. She'd never touched a man this way, and she couldn't help but react to it. Her palm tingled, her skin heated and her heart began to race.

R.J.'s chest lifted and fell with a deep, shuddering breath, and for a single moment, his eyes closed. Then he pulled her hand away. Rather than let her go, he slid his hand from her wrist and laced their fingers together.

His voice was little more than a rasping rumble, his eyes narrowed dangerously, when he explained, "Just so you know."

She blinked at him as he turned, then tugged her toward the house. Like a sleepwalker, she followed his lead. Their hands were pressed together, trapping the male heat of him against her palm.

He didn't look at her as they walked. "You may not know a hell of a lot about men, honey, but you've got to know enough to understand an erection. I want you, plain and simple. Remember that the next time you accuse me of something."

"I'm...I'm sorry." She didn't know what else she could say. She was still reeling from the realization that he'd wanted her and that he'd given up—at least for the moment.

R.J. groaned, then his muscles relaxed. He flashed her a crooked grin over his shoulder. "Don't be. Your first assumption was right, too. I *do* want control, and by God, I'll have it."

CHAPTER NINE

THEY FOUGHT all day long.

R.J. couldn't remember a time when he'd had this much trouble making someone—especially a woman—see things his way. Everyone tended to agree with him. Eventually. He had been raised, and was accepted, as the oldest son of the Maitland family. He was the president of Maitland Maternity, a world-renowned center. He was sought after by debutantes from miles around. Clout was his middle name, and he used it without thought whenever he deemed it necessary.

But Dana had spent the day defying him on even the simplest requests, which marked a complete turnaround for her.

She was usually so obliging with him, handling even the most monumental tasks with extra care just to please him. It was what he was used to from her. It was what he expected. Now she seemed to have developed an uncommon use of the word *no*. And it didn't matter what he did, she held firm.

Between wanting her and being flatly denied, and having everything he offered thrown back in his face, his normally healthy ego was badly battered. Women seldom told him no, and he couldn't recall the last time he'd had a gift refused.

He glanced at Dana's profile as he pulled the Mercedes into the drive and strove for a calm he was far from feeling. Dana, as usual, looked cool as an arctic blast. It was an expression he once appreciated but now resented. "You're being unreasonable."

She didn't look at him, just stared straight ahead at the house. "Because I don't want you to give me a credit card when I already have two of my own?"

Her look clearly said he was the one being unreasonable. Not that he cared. "That's hardly the point, Dana."

She pressed on, her tone irritatingly clipped and formal. "Because I don't want a joint savings account when we each already have our own?" She cast him a quick look. "And R.J., you pay me well. My accounts are not in need of padding."

She was being deliberately obtuse, but he didn't say so. A joint account would allow him to supply her with some of his own money, money he could well afford to spare. He needed to do *something* for her, to reciprocate her generosity in some way, but she turned him down every damn time he tried.

"Stop squeezing the steering wheel, R.J. You're going to break it in two."

R.J. glared at her and saw she was glaring right back. The cool detachment was gone. Her green eyes looked as if they were lit from within, something he'd never witnessed in Dana. There were a lot of things about her he'd never noticed before—muleheaded stubbornness, for one.

He'd thought the long ride would have given her time to think, but she hadn't calmed down at all. She was prepared to reject him on every level.

He took some measure of satisfaction in seeing the chain around her neck and the ring on her finger. She wore the bracelet, too, though he couldn't detect it beneath her sleeve.

She'd accepted precious little from him, but the possessive part of him was mollified to see that in at least some small way, he'd been able to please her.

He pulled into the garage and shoved the car into park. Now, if he could just get her to agree on a few more things…. "Having an account in both our names—"

"Will make you feel like you're paying me for marrying you." Her words rang with outrage, which appeared to have shocked her as well as him. After a moment, she gave a melodramatic sigh and dropped her head back against the seat. "R.J., I've already told you it wasn't necessary to buy my help. I don't want your credit cards. I don't want your money."

She doesn't want me. He shook that thought off just as quickly as he realized it. He didn't particularly *want* her to want him; the marriage was temporary, and once it was over, he hoped things could go back—to some degree—to the way they'd been before.

He knew deep in his gut they'd never be exactly the

same again. Not after he'd kissed her. And touched her. Not after he'd been buried deep inside her and found out he was the only one.

Not after he'd given her the impression he was a totally uncontrolled, bumbling fool in the sack. He felt disgustingly embarrassed every time he thought of it, and that made him angry, too.

He didn't really blame Dana for not wanting to give him a second chance. It had been her first time, and he'd totally lost control. He hadn't gently seduced her as he'd originally planned. He hadn't left her utterly sated when he walked away to go to his own room.

No, he'd left her hiding out in the bathroom after giving her nothing but a taste of how a wild man might behave.

Dana was controlled, always poised, always elegant. Sweaty, gritty sex likely repulsed her—especially since he'd been in such a frenzy to have her, she hadn't even gotten to climax.

R.J. swore softly, then threw open his door. Dana climbed out on her own, refusing to let him open her door the way a gentleman should, the way he wanted to. *Damn woman.*

The whole day was frustrating, and getting more so by the minute. After they'd tidied up the breakfast dishes together, he'd taken her on a tour of the house. She'd been woefully unimpressed, though she'd made appropriate noises of appreciation. But he knew her better than that. It was the plants, and especially the pond, that she found fascinating. They'd spent several hours outside, just walking and talking. Even in her enthusiasm, Dana had tried to remain impersonal. But he'd now met the woman beneath the suit. He knew what she tasted like, the way she sounded when she was sexually aroused. He knew the heated scents of her body.

Damn, if only he'd taken his time. She'd been satisfyingly close for a while there—until he'd botched it.

Dana headed into the house, oblivious to his heated thoughts, and R.J. made note of the gentle sway of her hips. Trailing behind her would become a new hardship, given she wanted a hands-off relationship. He was only too aware of how wonderfully touchable she was. He swallowed hard. "Where are you off to?"

"I'm going to make a few calls."

She kept walking, not bothering to look back. R.J. reached out and snagged the back of her shirt, pulling her up short. "What kind of calls?"

Looking over her shoulder, she glanced first at his face, then the fist holding her in place. One brow rose in the same imperious manner Megan often used. It was a command, plain and simple.

It wasn't easy, but R.J. managed to loosen his fingers and let her go. He shoved his hands into his pockets to resist the urge to grab her again.

"First I'm going to have my car driven over here."

That brought him up short. He hadn't even considered her car. "Why?"

"We have work tomorrow, remember?"

He remembered only too well. His mother had given him grief for not taking Dana on a honeymoon. She hadn't been impressed with his explanation of sudden decisions, bad timing and set schedules. Megan knew he could rearrange things if he chose to, just as she knew he'd damn well take a honeymoon if that was what he wanted to do.

But a honeymoon had never been the purpose of the marriage.

"I can drive you to work. We're going to the same place."

"I'd rather have my own car."

"Then we can get it later in the week."

She gave him a pensive frown. "Our schedules seldom mesh, R.J., other than arriving close to the same time. But I generally like to get there before you—"

"You don't need to do that now."

She shook her head. "Work is work, and I won't let our pretend marriage change that. Besides, you often stay later than I do and have meetings after hours when I go home. You're what we normal people call a workaholic. If you had to chauffeur me around, you'd resent it."

She had a point, not that he'd admit it. "I hardly think driving my wife somewhere could be called chauffeuring."

"Your *pretend* wife."

"To the world it's real."

"And to the real world, it makes sense for us to drive

separate cars." Irritation edged into her tone. "I know for a fact you have meetings planned for lunch most of this week, while I usually meet one of my friends. We need two cars, so I might as well get mine here tonight. Besides, I've already made arrangements with my neighbor to have it dropped off. All I need to do is let him know."

R.J. ran a hand through his hair. Frustration gnawed at him, but he couldn't say exactly why. Two days ago, he'd have been insistent that she have her own car, because that would have guaranteed his freedom. Now he saw it as another tactic on her part to put distance between them. She wanted as little to do with him as possible, and his ego naturally rebelled. He'd expected to be the one fending her off, not the other way around.

He dropped his hands. "Fine. You want to drive yourself, you can use my Mercedes. I'll drive the Explorer—"

She stared at him. "You have an Explorer?"

"I use it when I travel or when I go to the lake."

"Oh." Then she shook her head. "R.J, I have my *own* car, thank you. I don't need yours."

A smart man always knew when to retreat, which meant he was losing his edge because he should have stopped ten minutes ago. "All right. Is that all you have to do now?"

"No. I'm going to set up some damage control. That's why we got married in the first place, remember?"

If he threw her over his shoulder and hauled her

upstairs, would she fight him? Probably. Dana didn't appear to have an amicable bone left in her entire body— at least not where he was concerned. "It's Sunday. How much organizing can you do today?"

"Plenty. This is the best time to start because everyone will be home. I'm going to get the ball rolling on our public announcement, just in case the papers haven't gotten wind of it yet. And this coming week we're going to make the rounds visiting some of the places you regularly donate to. Like the One Way Farm for kids, the women's shelter, the various medical research facilities. You're very generous with your time and money, but no one reports on that."

He eyed her mutinous, disgruntled expression and knew she was feeling defensive on his behalf again. It was a unique experience having someone champion him, though he realized now that Dana had always done exactly that, so subtly that he'd barely noticed. He didn't like knowing that he'd taken her for granted, that he'd appreciated only part of the woman she was. "Don't get riled, honey. I doubt anyone even knows what I donate or to whom."

"Exactly." She raised a small fist. "But if the press wants to hound you this week, well, they can just follow us around and give some added publicity to the charities that need it. In fact, that'll be your stand, okay?"

Besides making him hot, she amused the hell out of him. "My stand?"

She began pacing as she pulled her thoughts together.

"You want to turn all the bad publicity into some good. You don't mind being in the limelight if it will help someone. In fact, you welcome the press!" She nodded in satisfaction at her own conclusions, then turned away. "I'm going to get started on this right now."

R.J. stood there, speechless. Dana was in full work mode, so there was no point getting in her way. She went into *his* den and shut the door with a click, firmly closing him out.

Muttering a muffled oath, R.J. went down the hall. The night would arrive soon enough, and he'd try reasoning with her again.

It was a strange reaction on his part, because making love with a virgin had never appealed to him before. The few inexperienced women he'd known hadn't been very satisfactory lovers. They hadn't been virgins, but neither had they known enough to fully reciprocate his sensual advances. He'd done all the work, gotten little enough in the way of response, and there'd been no giving, no real sharing.

With Dana, it had been different. Her response had been first shyly open, then blindly feverish. She'd been more than willing to give and take, holding nothing back from him—until he'd lost control.

R.J. bit the side of his mouth, remembering the hot, tight clasp of her body as he'd pushed his way into her, the wetness, the seductive scent of her arousal. He got hard just thinking about it.

Damn, would he ever be given a second chance?

He thumped his fist against his thigh, cursing low and making a silent vow. Tonight, he'd get started on wearing her down. He'd be honest with her, telling her that she'd turned him on, explaining why he'd lost control and promising it wouldn't happen again. No woman could resist a well-phrased compliment, especially when it was true. And just maybe she'd appreciate the fact that he'd found her so desirable he'd been pushed over the edge when no other woman had had that effect on him.

No, he decided abruptly, he'd keep that part to himself. No reason to leave himself so open or to make her think she had more influence on him than she did. Their marriage was temporary, after all, and he didn't want her to start imagining things that could never be.

All he really had to do was show her that he was no slacker in bed, that the rumors of him being a good lover hadn't been false, contrary to what she'd witnessed. He had to prove to her that her first plan hadn't been a bad one after all. And he had to make her understand that she could have incredible pleasure with him.

He had to have her, period.

DANA WAS SATISFIED with all she'd accomplished. She'd spoken to many of R.J.'s relatives, as well as some family acquaintances and closer friends. She'd given her humble apologies for not inviting them to the wedding, but claimed that under the circumstances, she and R.J. had wanted as little publicity as possible. Everyone had been gracious enough to say they understood, though she knew his sisters were hurt, especially Anna.

Though R.J. felt fully a part of Megan's family and was accepted and loved as the oldest brother, there remained a special bond between him and Anna.

Anna had only been a few months old when their father had abandoned the two of them. R.J. wasn't a demonstrative man, but his protectiveness and affection for Anna and her son, Will, were apparent to anyone who'd ever seen them together.

Dana had left the special circumstances of their marriage for R.J. to explain to Anna. He could tell her as much or as little as he decided was appropriate. Dana had never had any close relatives of her own except for her mother, who had passed away years ago, so she couldn't begin to fully understand, much less interfere with, their special relationship.

It was getting late when she finished making her plans for the week and had jotted down notes on things to do for the next day. She'd made a good head start on her intentions, but the week promised to be a hectic one. Since she was privy to R.J.'s schedule, she had taken the liberty of filling almost every available minute with an eye to repairing his reputation. That was the one thing she could do for him, and she was determined it would work.

Her car was dropped off and she paid her neighbor, who'd obligingly agreed to the service, before he took a cab home. Dana wondered about R.J.'s stubbornness concerning the cars, but little of what he'd done since the marriage could have been predicted based on what she knew about him—and she'd thought she knew him well.

Dana didn't see R.J. as she made her way upstairs to take a shower and get ready for bed. She was actually relieved. She didn't relish running into him again, rehashing all the reasons she couldn't accept his money. True, she didn't have his wealth, but she was comfortable. You didn't work as the executive secretary for R.J. Maitland without getting well paid for it. But even if she'd been a pauper, she'd never have let him pay her for their marriage.

Her pride, which he'd yet to discover rivaled his own, wouldn't allow for such a thing.

She went to her room, idly wondering where R.J. had gotten to. Maybe he'd already retired for the night. Bone tired herself, she kicked off her shoes and stripped off her slacks, putting them neatly away. Then she turned to the mirror and pulled the pins from her hair. She was just reaching for the hem of her tunic to pull it over her head when there was a brisk knock on the dividing door and it opened.

Dana turned to stone.

A frozen, heavy silence filled the room. She could only imagine how she looked, standing there in nothing more than a long shirt, her hair disheveled, bordering on wild since she'd yet to pull a brush through it.

And R.J. He stood there staring, one hand still on the

doorknob, one foot inside the room. His hazel eyes were fixed on her, not wavering the tiniest bit, and she could see the slow clenching of his jaw, could feel the strange energy gathering around him like a brewing storm.

Awkwardness swamped her, and she reached up to smooth her hair, though she knew it wouldn't do a bit of good. As if that movement had galvanized him, R.J. stepped the rest of the way into the room and shut the door behind him. He didn't say a word as he strolled barefoot across the carpet to stand directly in front of her.

There was an intense light in his eyes, turning the hazel to gold, and a frown marred his brow. His gaze slid with excruciating slowness over her, from the top of her head to the tips of her toes, lingering for long moments on her exposed legs.

Dana shifted her feet, pressing her knees together. Through the lump in her throat, she choked out the words that needed to be said. "I'd appreciate it if you didn't just barge in here."

It was as if she hadn't spoken. "Damn, you have beautiful hair."

She was too stunned to even blush. She simply wanted him out of the room before he felt forced to offer more outrageous compliments. "R.J., I'm in the middle of changing clothes." Her hands shook, and she tugged ineffectually on the bottom of the tunic, trying to stretch the material to cover her thighs.

His gaze met hers, and she felt seared by the heat.

"I'm glad I didn't wait. You'd have never let me in, not looking like this."

"You're right." She started to step away, but she refused to be a coward. Situations such as this were bound to occur sooner or later. Though it was painfully awkward—at least for her—now was the perfect time to resolve them, so future incidents could be avoided.

The fact that he kept staring at her legs made it even more difficult. Men didn't look at her with such intensity, and certainly R.J. never had. In fact, she couldn't remember any man ever seeing her legs before. The skirts she favored were long, ending just below her knees. Besides, her legs were unexceptional. They were thin, long, pale. Not the shapely tanned legs of a beach bunny.

She did her best to stand still. "R.J., you promised me my privacy when I agreed to the marriage."

Other than drawing his darkened gaze from her legs to her face, he ignored her. She knew R.J. had a knack of forcing the topic any way he chose, and this was no different. Still, she was speechless when he reached out and tangled his fist in her hair.

"You look like a siren." His fist moved, his fingers caressing. "Your hair is so damn soft and sexy."

"R.J., please." This time she did try to step away, but since he didn't let go of her hair, she was drawn up short with a wince.

He didn't appear to notice. "And your legs." His free hand settled on her hip, his fingers gently squeezing as he looked down the length of her. "You have world-class legs, babe. I had no idea."

Her breath came too fast as she frantically tried to think of a way to get him out of the room.

"I keep thinking about last night," he continued. "How soft and sweet you were under me. I couldn't see you then. Damn, if I had, I wouldn't have lasted as long as I did, and we both know it wasn't nearly long enough."

As if that statement had reminded him of something, he jerked his gaze to her face. "You made me crazy. I hadn't expected that. Usually I'm controlled, and I can keep the lovemaking going for hours. I enjoy watching a woman climax, hearing her cry out, feeling her tighten around me."

His breath, coming in low, rough gusts, brushed her temple as he leaned closer, nuzzling against her. "That's what I meant to do with you," he whispered, the words a soft stirring of air in her ear, making her skin tingle and her toes curl. "You took me by surprise."

His hand tightened on her hip, and he drew her close so she could feel the length of his erection against her abdomen. "I put my fingers inside you, and you were so damn wet—"

Dana jerked away with a gasp, taking several steps across the room until she was safely on the other side of the bed. She hadn't known men talked this way, that they said things so bluntly. Or maybe it was just R.J., his natural arrogance in always speaking his mind.

"Don't," she rasped, the words raw and shaky. "Don't say dumb things just to manipulate me, to get the upper hand."

R.J. looked poleaxed. He stood there, one hand still outstretched, his chest rising and falling, twin slashes of color high on his cheekbones. Very slowly, he lowered his hand to his side. *"Dumb* things?"

Dana felt close to losing her composure completely. She didn't want R.J. to see her like this, half clothed, vulnerable, behaving like a fool. If she expected to keep working with him after the marriage ended, she had to keep their relationship as normal as possible. He'd never wanted her emotions to interfere in the past. She had to believe he'd want it even less now.

She drew a deep breath and searched for control. R.J. had always liked and respected her for her reasonableness, her common sense. She dredged that up now, trying to sound cavalier. "I...I know what I look like, R.J. I'm levelheaded, not silly. And I've long since resigned myself to being plain. It's not something that bothers me."

His frown came slowly, not a frown of intensity, but one of building anger. His tone was low and rough, each word carefully enunciated. "You are not plain."

She laughed, though she felt far from amused. She refused to let him see how the topic of her very ordinary appearance hurt her. "I have mirrors, R.J. And I'm neither blind nor delusional. In fact, I'd say I'm rather astute."

"On occasion, usually with business," he agreed. "But this time you're dead wrong. Or are you going to stand there and call me a liar?"

She hadn't expected such a strong attack. She cleared her throat, wondering how to defuse this little disagreement—bizarre as it seemed—and get him out of her room.

"I wouldn't call it lying, exactly." She watched him, trying to calculate his reaction to her honesty. "More like outrageous flattery, something we both know you're an expert at when it suits you. But I'm not a woman easily fooled and the flattery is unnecessary anyway, since we've both agreed not to continue in any sort of... sexual intimacy."

"I didn't agree to a damn thing. And after seeing you like this, you can bet your sweet behind I want to get intimate. I want to get real intimate." He advanced on her, slowly circling the bed while keeping her pinned with his icy gaze. "I want to see the rest of you, Dana, not just your legs, which really are sexy as sin."

She shook her head, mute.

"I want you naked from head to toe. I want to see the breasts I held and touched and kissed last night. And your nipples. Do you know your whole body shuddered when I sucked on your nipples?"

Dana found herself speechless. She'd never dealt with R.J. in a mood like this and had no idea how to handle him. And she'd never in her wildest dreams imagined hearing anything so outrageous and bold said to her.

She'd truly had no idea men spoke in such a way, not even R.J.

She bit her lip, more unsure of herself as a woman than ever before.

R.J.'s eyes narrowed when she remained silent, then focused intently on her mouth. His voice dropped another octave until it was so low she could barely hear him.

"I want to feel those long legs of yours around my waist. And I want to watch your face when I enter you, this time with no surprises. It'll be easier, you know. I'll make damn sure there's no discomfort."

Her heart beat so hard she felt it throughout her entire body.

R.J.'s smile was both gentle and predatory. "Most of all," he growled, "I want to watch your beautiful eyes when I give you your first orgasm."

"R.J." Dana tried to retreat a step. She bumped up against the bed and nearly tumbled onto it, only gaining her balance at the last second.

R.J. caught her arms in a gentle, unbreakable hold. "I have no idea why in hell you're so set on calling yourself plain or why you've tried to convince the rest of the world the same damn thing, but you're wrong." He gave her a slight shake to emphasize his statement. "Now that I've seen you, I don't intend to let you continue hiding from me."

"I was never hiding." She pressed against his chest, but he was as unmovable as an oak tree.

"Then what would you call it?"

"Being…being realistic." She took a breath and tried to explain before things got further out of hand. Had R.J. misunderstood and taken her actions as a challenge? She had to set him straight. "I've accepted who I am, how I look. I don't need you to dress things up for me."

R.J. seemed to consider that, his expression so piercing she felt herself squirm under his regard. His hands softened and began idly caressing her, then he lifted one hand to her cheek and smoothed her messed hair. "Let's sit down a minute and talk."

The only place for them both to sit was on the mattress, and she'd already determined never to find herself there with him again. "No, I…I want to get ready for bed."

His grin was fleeting. "Bed was uppermost on my mind when I came in here, at least until I understood just how damn confused you are."

He drew her down next to him on the edge of the mattress and kept hold of her hand, his fingers toying with hers, as if he needed the moment to measure his words. Finally he looked at her, and his smile was boyishly crooked and wickedly sensual. "If I'd seen you like this before," he said, "you'd never have lasted so long as my assistant."

"Why not?" Dana wasn't certain what to think, and with every word R.J. confused her further.

"Because I'd have had to make love with you. And office romances never last."

Her heart squeezed tight in pain. Was this his way of telling her that once the marriage was over, so was their business association?

"Is that why you hid from me? So we wouldn't get involved?"

Dana shook her head. R.J.'s eyes flared, and he caught her chin, halting her automatic protest. She met his gaze reluctantly. "I never hid from you."

"Then it's yourself you're hiding from." Taking her totally off guard, he slid his hand from her chin to her breast, cuddling her softly in his palm.

Dana gasped, frozen in place, and R.J. gave a soft groan. "You see, you're very much a woman." He moved his hand to her other breast and treated it to the same torment, allowing his fingers to find and stroke her nipple. Even through her bra and shirt, the feeling was exquisite and she bit her lip hard.

"Shh. Don't do that. Don't freeze up on me. I'm not going to rush you, babe, I promise. Last night was a mistake, an aberration for me. Next time will be so much better. You have my word on that. But I've been going crazy wanting you again, and now I'm finally starting to understand a few things."

His fingers continued to tease and stroke, and she could barely think straight. "What things?"

"Number one, that you have no idea of your appeal. What I want to know is why."

"R.J., I—"

His hand gently squeezed her breast in sensual

warning, his body going still. "Don't say it, Dana." His words were a muttered command, not harsh, but more compelling for their quiet. "Don't sit there and tell me how unattractive you are, because I won't let you lie to me or yourself."

It was difficult to breathe, difficult to form a coherent argument. Her breasts ached, as did other parts of her body. Without thinking, she leaned into his taunting palm and slowly closed her eyes. "I've always been plain, from the time I was a little girl."

He smoothed her breast without missing a beat. "Says who?"

At first she didn't hear the suppressed rage in his tone, she was so overwhelmed by sensations. His nearness, the heat from his large body, his heady, masculine scent. But she did hear it, and her reply was duly cautious. "My…my mother was a practical woman. She saw no reason why I should waste my time trying to be something I could never be."

His curse was low and filled with such fury she shuddered in response. Why was he so angry?

"Where's your mother now?"

He released her breast, making her sigh in relief—and disappointment. His hands tightened on her, one wrapping securely around her fingers, trapping her hand on his hard thigh, while the other slipped over her shoulders to draw her flush against his side.

Dana didn't dare look at him, too unsure of what she

would see and of what she was feeling. "She passed away several years ago."

"I didn't know."

"There was no reason you should have. My mother moved to northern Oklahoma once I started to work, to a small town there." She peeked at him, then quickly away. She felt like a fainthearted ninny, but so much had happened that she'd never experienced before, she had no way of knowing how to deal with it. "We hadn't been close for a long time, but I saw her on holidays and during my vacations. In fact, I used one of my vacations to go home and take care of the arrangements after she died unexpectedly."

She could feel the tension emanating from him. "How did it happen?"

A vague uneasiness had filtered into his tone that she didn't understand. "She had a massive stroke. By the time I was notified, she was already gone."

There was a stretch of painful silence before R.J. asked, "Why didn't you tell me?"

She looked at him and said simply, "You don't pay me to involve you in my personal affairs. I asked for the time off, and you gave it to me."

He left the bed in an angry rush. "I've been a bastard."

"No!" Dana jumped to her feet and caught his arm. She held tight, though he didn't try to pull away. "That's not true, R.J. You're one of the most generous, giving men I've ever known."

"Yeah, right. That's why after years of employment, after being friends with my family and with me, you never bothered to tell me when your mother passed away."

He sounded hurt, and she stared at him, bewildered. "I don't understand why you care."

He turned to face her. "Where's your father?"

Dana lifted one shoulder. She didn't know why he was pushing so hard on this. "I have no idea. I never knew the man."

R.J. looked her over, and she was acutely aware of her position at the side of the bed, her feet together, her knees together, her hands clasped at her waist. She was on the verge of pulling the spread from the bed and whipping it around her when he asked, "Will you explain that?"

"If you really want to know."

He crossed his arms over his chest, planted his feet apart and waited. He wouldn't leave her room until he was good and ready, she decided. "My father left my mother for another woman when I was still a baby. She said it was some awful floozy who was much younger than him."

"A pretty woman?"

"I suppose. Surely he wouldn't have run off with a homely woman."

R.J. worked his jaw in thought. "So you have no memory of your father at all?"

"No. There weren't even any pictures since my

mother destroyed them all. But she told me often that I took after him in my looks."

His eyes narrowed. "How so?"

"He had the same washed-out hair color, the same thin, lanky build."

A savage sound escaped him. "I take it she was a bitter woman?"

She didn't want R.J. to know about her painful relationship with her mother, how hard she had found it to tolerate her mother's critical nature and jaded outlook. As soon as she'd been old enough, she'd put space between them, but she'd never shared the hurt with anyone and didn't want to start now.

Keeping all emotion out of her tone, she said, "Oh, yes, Mother was angry. To hear her tell it, my father was a loathsome creature with no scruples at all. I got the feeling the woman he ran off with wasn't his first indiscretion." Then she added, "He hurt her very badly, leaving her alone with a baby to raise."

"With *you* to raise."

She nodded. "Yes."

R.J. seemed to be soaking it all in, and he didn't look pleased. Dana decided it was time to change the subject.

"I called your family earlier to explain about our wedding."

His head jerked up and his eyes glittered. "You told them—"

"No! No, I didn't tell them that. How you explain

things to your family is your business. I just told them that because of all the bad publicity that had been circulating and because you knew they all had plenty on their minds, you'd wanted to keep things as simple as possible."

He grunted, and she wasn't sure if it was a sound of favor or disapproval.

Dana nervously fiddled with the hem on her shirt. She was in a bedroom with the man she'd loved forever, her hair in wild disarray, and wearing only half her clothes. All things considered, she thought she was handling the situation well. "Do you know what Abbey told me?"

"That she'd have my ass for not inviting her?"

Dana chuckled despite her uneasiness. R.J. teased and bantered with all his sisters, but they knew he loved them just the same. "No. She said you were far too upstanding to shirk your responsibilities. It angers her that you've been put through this mess."

"It hasn't been easy for anyone involved."

"No, it hasn't. But you're the one the press has been pointing a finger at most."

R.J. had been pacing, and suddenly he stopped. Hands on his hips, head tilted, he studied her, then suddenly laughed. "I'll be damned. You did that deliberately, didn't you?"

She stared at him, surprised by his sudden mood shift. "What?"

"Changed the subject on me. We were talking about

you and your personal misconceptions, not about me and this bloody scandal."

Dana laced her hands together and lifted her chin. "The scandal will die down once I get through pointing out—truthfully—what an outstanding person you are. I've got a busy week planned for you, and I trust you won't complain."

R.J. shook his head. "No, you don't. I'm not letting you lead me off the track that easily again. I'm on to you now, lady."

Dana didn't want him to be on to her. She didn't want him delving into her psyche, picking away at her painful past. Her childhood hadn't been an easy one, and now R.J. wanted to refute what she knew as truth. But it was so much easier to cling to her old beliefs than to take a chance on believing in him.

R.J. didn't appear willing to give her a choice in the matter. He looked her over once more and smiled. "Sometimes my own stupidity amazes me."

"You are *not* stupid, R.J."

"I'm not a bad lover, either, but I suppose I'll have to prove it."

"No!"

He started toward her again, this time with a purpose. "I think the only way to make you understand just how attractive I find you is to show you. So that's what I'm going to do."

As he advanced again, she backed up. Only this time she moved too fast, and when she hit the edge of the bed she lost her balance and dropped back on it, bouncing twice.

R.J. was over her before she could even catch her breath.

CHAPTER TEN

R.J. LOOKED DOWN at her wide-eyed expression and smiled gently. "I'm not going to maul you, Dana. Relax."

She gave an audible gulp and stiffened even more.

"It's amazing," he half teased, "how different a woman can look after a man gets to know her."

"You've known me for years!"

"No, I've known the woman you've pretended to be, not the real you." And now he thought he knew why she'd always hidden herself. Dana had bought into her mother's angry words. Her mother claimed Dana looked a lot like her father—and the father was a total bastard. How had that made Dana feel?

"Is that what you think?" she asked, her voice unnaturally high. "That I'm now somehow different? Just because you've caught me with my hair loose and my..." Her words trailed off.

"And your pants off?" His grin was wicked, but then, he felt wicked. Wicked and eager. Patience had never been his virtue, but in this case he'd find a healthy dose of it somewhere. Dana needed to learn her own appeal, and he intended to instruct her on the matter. There'd be no reason for him to dent his pride, not when he had a perfect excuse for getting closer to her. "I'd like to get the rest of your clothes off, too."

"No!"

"I wish I could remove that damn word from your vocabulary." He wanted to reassure her, to help her relax. He had no intention of rushing her now that he realized how much care she needed, not only because of her virginity, but because of her fragile ego. "Regardless of my animalistic display of yesterday, I am capable of controlling my baser instincts. I want you. Ever since I stepped in here and saw your bare legs and your hair loose and the warm blush on your face, all I've thought about is making love with you. But I don't want you to be afraid of me—"

"I'm not afraid of you." She looked appalled at the mere suggestion.

"—and I don't want you to be nervous. I want you to trust me."

Very softly, she whispered, "I do trust you, R.J. That's not what this is about. It's…it's a lot more complicated than that."

R.J. felt a lick of dread go down his spine. He stiffened, feeling the tension gather in his neck. "You want me to have a paternity test done?"

Dana looked at him blankly. "What?"

He gently smoothed his hand over her hair, though he felt anything but gentle. "You're still wondering if maybe I'm the father of the baby, aren't you?"

He braced himself for her reply, but wasn't ready for her burst of anger. She shoved him, almost throwing him to the side. He caught her shoulders and held her still. "Dana?"

Hands pressed flat on his chest, she lifted her head and shouted an inch from his nose, "No! I do not think you're the baby's father. That's a stupid thing for you to say. For the last time, R.J., anyone who knows you knows it's an utterly ridiculous accusation."

The emotions that hit him then were too confusing to sort out. Her belief in him meant a lot, and he was grateful for it. But if the paternity issue wasn't the problem, then he'd been right all along.

He'd been a failure in the sack. He felt the heat of his embarrassment climb up his neck. She didn't want to sleep with him again not because she doubted his honor, but because he'd been such a disappointment. His expertise in pleasing a woman had never been questioned before now.

Of course, he'd never gone deaf, dumb and blind over a woman before, either.

He clenched his teeth and resisted the urge to defend himself once again. Dana was simply too inexperienced and too unsure of her own appeal to understand that it was his hunger for her that had driven him wild. All she knew was that he'd come after her with the finesse of a rutting bulldog, and she hadn't found any satisfaction at all.

That thought made his muscles twitch. He couldn't

wait to bring Miss Dana Maitland—his wife—to completion, to show her in explicit detail just how appealing she really was. Once she found out what sex was all about, things would be different between them.

But in the meantime, he needed to work at shoring up her confidence. He had no doubt her mother had played a real number on her, repressing Dana's natural sensuality as something evil. After all, it was the sensuality of some other woman that had taken her husband away.

It was ironic that Dana's father had abandoned her because he didn't care about his wife, while R.J.'s father had walked away because his wife had died, leaving him a man incapable of caring about anyone or anything else.

He held her head between his hands, keeping her gaze locked with his. He enjoyed looking at her, and his fascination with her emerald eyes hadn't diminished one bit. He smoothed his thumbs over her cheekbones, seemingly unable to stop touching her. His sweet, efficient, orderly Dana.

She was by far the sexiest woman he'd ever seen.

"I've never in my adult life," he whispered, "treated a woman the way I did you last night. But it was your fault too, honey. You shocked the hell out of me. I didn't expect you to be so…"

"So what?" Her antagonistic tone proved she was going to fight him every inch of the way. "I'm just me, R.J. The same woman you've known for years, the woman you recognized for her secretarial skills. Not for anything else."

She was so defensive, he thought. He had his work cut out for him. R.J. rolled to the side and then hauled her up in the bed so they were lying against the pillows. "Let's look at this logically." He lifted a long strand of her hair and examined it. "You have beautiful hair, soft and pale. Not at all washed out. That's just plain stupid. Look at it, Dana, how the light catches it. It's the type of hair a man imagines spread out over his pillow while his woman smiles up at him."

"I already told you flattery doesn't affect me."

He hid a grin. Her voice had shaken just the tiniest bit as she made that statement. R.J. propped himself up on one elbow. Without moving a single inch, Dana looked at him. She had the appearance of a frightened doe, too wary to move but too cautious not to keep a close eye on him. Her body was rigid.

"What color was your mother's hair?"

"She had very thick, dark brown hair."

"I see." And he did. He could imagine her mother making all kinds of comparisons, but he held his anger in check. Dana didn't need his anger now.

Once again, he settled his palm over her breast. "Mmm. So soft. Those suits you wear make it impossible for a man to see what's beneath. But now I've felt you, and I've tasted you, and I know." He met her wide, unblinking gaze. "I won't ever forget, babe."

As he continued to touch her, her lips parted on a

shuddering breath. He didn't want to overly arouse her, because he wanted her to know he'd wait for her. Until she told him she wanted him, until she began to believe in herself, he'd settle for giving her all the compliments she hadn't gotten from him so far.

"Do you want me, Dana?"

Her lashes fluttered as if she was trying to regain her wits. "You didn't marry me for this."

He rested his hand on her silky thigh and wanted to shout out how much he wanted her. But that sure as hell wouldn't reassure her. "We could consider it an added benefit."

He said it like a question, leaving the ball in her court. Part of him was so turned on he felt as if he could come with just a touch. He couldn't recall ever wanting a woman so badly or denying himself so completely.

But another part of him, the natural protector, wanted to hold her close and dispel whatever ridiculous myth her mother had perpetrated. Why would any mother make her daughter believe such nonsense?

Dana shyly reached up and put her small palm on his chest. Just that, such a simple touch, and his guts tightened in reaction. She looked at him, her eyes dark and soft, her lashes leaving shadows on her cheekbones. He kissed her nose.

"R.J., I like my job."

"I'm glad." He was distracted by her small ears, tracing the gentle whorls with a fingertip.

"If you and I…if we had sex…"

"Yes." Hell yes.

"...it would change everything."

R.J. stalled in the middle of licking her ear. Damn. That had been his argument from the first, but he no longer cared. Somewhere along the way his common sense had been sidelined by other emotions, and they were totally different from the physical wanting that had exploded inside him. There was tenderness and curiosity and a deep caring. He'd known Dana for many years and naturally felt a unique fondness for her, built on in part by her loyalty and commitment to the job. That fondness had suddenly altered into something else, though, something he wasn't entirely certain of. All he knew was that he wanted her to be aware of her feminine charms, to know that he wanted her because of the woman she was, not because of a duty he felt from her initial demands or an enforced closeness.

Lifting his head to look at her, he asked carefully, "What if I promise you I won't let it interfere with your job?"

She snorted. "That'd be impossible, even for you."

He rubbed her thigh and felt her shift subtly against him. Damn, he wanted to rip that awful, baggy tunic off her and kiss her whole luscious body. He sucked in a lungful of air and said, "You're right, of course. I'm sorry." He took her hand and carried it to his erection, holding her fingers tight against him while watching her eyes widen. "I'm afraid a man's libido sometimes leaves no room for scruples. We'll say anything to convince a desirable female to see things our way, especially when in a state like the one I'm in now."

Her gaze remained glued to his face, and her fingers didn't move. She licked her lips. "Maybe… maybe it's that…um, state, that makes you think you want me."

He laughed, then groaned when her fingers tightened. "Sweetheart, you're the one who put me in this state, and I want you, not anyone else. Do you think I walk around like this all the time?"

"I don't know." Her expression turned serious, and her fingers started moving, gently squeezing him through his slacks, sliding the tiniest bit up and down his length, exploring. "I don't know much about this part of men."

He could barely talk. More than anything he wanted his pants off and her small hand on his naked flesh. His erection strained into her palm, and her eyes opened even wider.

"You moved."

R.J. choked. A fine beading of sweat touched his forehead. It took him a minute, but he managed to hold on to his control. He'd sooner become celibate than rush her again, and there was no way he'd stifle her curiosity. "You have your hand on me, sweetheart. It's driving me crazy. I moved."

"Oh." She started to pull away, but he caught her wrist.

"Crazy in an excruciatingly wonderful way." He saw

the awareness dawn in her eyes, saw her eyes darken, the pupils expand.

"Like this?" She stroked him with a tentative touch.

R.J. bit back a moan at the pleasure of it. "Yes." Then he added, "Harder."

Dana levered herself up on one arm, her reluctance forgotten. Rather than meet his eyes, she looked down at her hand, which curved around him through his slacks. She clenched her fingers, and when he jerked, she let him go. "Did I hurt you?"

"God, no," he rasped. "But I think we'd better stop right here or I'm a goner. I can't take much more."

"You can't?"

He shook his head. "No, absolutely not. That is, unless you want to carry things to the natural conclusion."

She stared at him, then scrambled to sit up. Before she turned her back to him, he saw her expression of dazed amazement. "I…no. I don't want us to…"

"Have sex." R.J. sat up, too, though more slowly. He took advantage of her distraction to straighten himself, then sighed with minimum relief. "That's where we were headed, you know."

She rubbed her forehead in confusion. "I don't know what got into me. I hadn't intended any of that."

R.J. looked at her straight, proud shoulders, her mussed hair, and grinned despite his painful arousal. "You're a woman and I'm a man and we want each other. Things are bound to get out of hand now and then."

Because he felt secure that she wouldn't be able to hold out against him for long, not with her natural sensuality, he said, "But don't worry. Until you make it clear that you want me, I won't pressure you."

She glanced at him over her shoulder, her expression one of complete disbelief.

Laughing, he flicked the tip of her nose. "I promise." But in the meantime, he'd also take advantage of his time with her to wear her down gently. He was thirty-nine years old; he knew women, and he knew how to get what he wanted. Before the week was out, Dana would be sleeping in his bed—where she belonged.

He gave her a swift, hard kiss good-night and forced himself to his feet. At the door, he stopped and faced her. "Good night, sweetheart. If you need anything, just let me know."

She still looked dazed by all that had transpired, but she managed a nod, and a polite, "Good night, R.J. Sleep well."

Ha. He'd be lucky if he slept at all with his body still on fire and the tempting knowledge that Dana, and relief, were only a few feet away. But while he lay awake, he'd have plenty to think on—like anticipating her surrender. He was a pro at getting what he wanted. Dana and all her silly hang-ups didn't stand a chance.

SHE WAS THE PRO—at sexual torment.

By Thursday, R.J. was wondering how much longer he'd be able to survive. He sat at his desk, ignoring the files Dana had just set before him. He wondered if it was his imagination or if she was deliberately teasing him. Lately, nothing with Dana was clear-cut. Oh, she still did the work of two people. More so than ever, in fact.

His mother had called just that afternoon to tell him he was once again in the papers. It had been that way every day, his face, his every word splashed across a multitude of papers from around the state. What wasn't a direct quote from a lucky source who'd been on the scene was taken from other reliable sources, because no one wanted to miss the story. He was big news.

The difference this time, of course, was that Dana had engineered the entire thing so he'd come off looking like a saint. There were photos of him holding babies at the clinic. Photos of him speaking with women from the shelter. Candid shots of him writing out a check to the One Way Farm for children, checks that were usually taken care of by his accountant.

And in fact, they *had* been taken care of already, not that he minded donating twice. He'd chosen the charities himself and wanted to do whatever he could to support them. It amused as well as irritated him that Dana wouldn't accept a single cent from him, but she had no problem giving his money away.

Dana had worked things perfectly, and now Austin society didn't know what to think. Was R. J. Maitland a man capable of abandoning his own child, or was he the great philanthropist?

R.J. didn't know what to think, either.

At that moment, Dana bustled in—there was no other word for her irritatingly cheery disposition in the face of his disgruntled frustration—and refilled his coffee cup. She wouldn't serve him at home, and in fact seemed to take exceptional glee in refusing him even the most minor gratuities, but at the office, nothing had changed.

The confounded woman knew he couldn't strip her naked at the office.

Though the thought had singular appeal.

After the cup was full, she perched her hip on the side of his desk, making his pulse quicken, and said, "R.J., Chelsea Markum just called. She wants to interview you."

He made a rude sound. "That conniving little bitch. What's she hoping to do? Negate all the headway you're making?"

Dana lifted a brow. "The headway *you're making.*"

He eyed the length of her legs, one bent at the knee and the other outstretched. Damn, but she had long legs. Killer legs. Why the hell had it taken him so long to notice?

Because the long, sturdy skirts she wore and the flat, ugly shoes on her feet conspired to hide that fact from everyone, including him.

He imagined her in a short, snug skirt—or better yet, no skirt at all. He took a deep, calming breath. "No one would have paid me the least attention these last few days if it hadn't been for you."

"Only because you're a private man and you consider your philanthropic tendencies no one's business but your own."

He leaned forward with a negligent lack of haste, his forearms flat on the desk, his hands close to her hip. One inch, he thought, and he'd be touching the soft curves of her behind.

She slipped off the desk to pace away.

R.J. swallowed his frustration. "My *tendencies* aren't anyone's business," he groused, "and if it hadn't been for Chelsea and her cutthroat newscast, things could have stayed that way."

Dana's gaze was suddenly solemn as she turned to him. "Oh, R.J." She searched his face. "Have I convinced you to do something you didn't want to do?"

After the miracles she'd performed, he felt like a cad. He left his seat and strode toward her. "Do you really think that's possible, babe?"

She blinked at the pet name he'd started to use and took one step back before halting and squaring her shoulders. "What?"

"For you to get me to do things I don't want to do?"

"Oh. Well, no, not really."

R.J. stood only three inches from her. Sunlight from the large window behind his desk poured over her, making her fair hair glint and gilding her eyelashes.

Her skin, he found, was incredible. Not a single flaw, just soft and silky and smooth. He wanted to explore that skin everywhere, on her belly, her upper thighs, the small of her back.

He made a low sound and took her shoulders in his hands. But as he lowered his head she ducked away, needlessly smoothing her hair as if he'd somehow mussed it.

"R.J., please," she whispered, glancing around, though they were alone in the big office. "We can't do that…here."

Evidently they couldn't do it anywhere. At least, not the *it* he wanted, which was everything. She let him kiss her occasionally and seemed to enjoy his attention. She even accepted the limited caress: a pat on the behind, a cuddle of her breast. The adolescent touches were enough to make him crazed. But if it went beyond that, if he started to breathe hard—which he seemed to do the second she responded to him—he'd see the haunting uncertainty cloud her big eyes.

His vow to wait until she was ready was wearing real thin.

She'd gone to his desk to straighten his papers, and he couldn't help himself. He stepped up behind her and slid his arms around her narrow waist, resting his jaw at the part of her hair on her crown. "Do you know what I've been thinking?" he murmured.

She was very still. "No."

"About you. And this damn enormous desk. And

how easy it would be to bend you over it." Her gasp was loud, but he was learning to read her, just barely, and he recognized the sound as mingled excitement and persistent reserve. "Like this."

He pressed his chest against her back and she automatically braced her hands flat, supporting her weight while bending forward. The position put her buttocks at a very interesting angle. He slid his hands down her rib cage until they were holding her hips, then let her feel how aroused he'd become already.

The insanity of need almost claimed him as he felt the soft, firm cushioning of her derriere against his hard flesh. His fingers contracted, and only by force of will did he make himself go slowly. With a more experienced woman, he'd already be driving deep, easing the hot need for them both.

Feather light, he kissed along the nape of her neck, which he'd learned was ultimately sensitive to his every touch. She shivered and made a small sound of surprised pleasure—a sound guaranteed to make him throb.

"Just a few buttons undone at your jacket and blouse, and I could be holding your naked breasts right now. Are your nipples hard, Dana?" The words and accompanying image affected him as much, if not more, than her. He groaned, then found out for himself that indeed they were. She was ripe, aching.

She pushed back against him in an instinctive search for relief when he lightly tugged at her pointed nipples.

His heart slammed against his rib cage. "Damn, but I love touching you, Dana."

She made a small sound, but R.J. couldn't be sure it was acceptance. He nipped her ear.

"If I pushed your skirt up high," he groaned against the side of her throat, "I could slide my hands between your soft thighs and—"

Straightening abruptly, she almost hit him in the head. She scrambled from between him and the desk. Chest heaving, eyes wide, face flushed, she stared up at him and blurted, "You have a meeting!"

"What?" Somehow that wasn't at all what he'd expected to hear. It took his sluggish brain a moment to assimilate the words.

Still panting, she closed her eyes as if that were the only way she could concentrate enough to speak coherently. Forming the words with care, she said, "You had a lunch meeting with Drake, remember?" She bit her lip, then opened her eyes. "He's…he's probably waiting for you right now."

R.J. stared at her, nonplussed, until the truth sank in.

Good God, he'd forgotten a meeting. The meeting had been penciled in on his calendar for over a week.

He remembered Dana putting the reminder note in front of him—and he'd watched the gentle sway of her shapely rump as she'd left.

He even remembered confirming with Drake earlier that very day—but his mind had been on Dana sitting primly at her desk, a sight visible through the open office doors.

In fact, he thought in numb horror as he looked at his desk piled with files he hadn't touched, he hadn't done a damn thing all day except think of her and let his imagination go wild. To be honest, the entire week had been pretty much a write-off. A sick tightening of his throat made it difficult to breathe, and he swallowed hard, then met Dana's nervous gaze.

His hands curled into fists. He was responsible, reputable, a self-professed workaholic, and that was how he liked it, damn it. Unlike his father, he didn't take his duties lightly. And as president of Maitland Maternity, a lot of people relied on him.

Something had to change.

He stepped around Dana and snatched his jacket from the desk chair. "Get on the phone with the restaurant. Have them tell Drake I was detained but I'm on my way."

She didn't answer, and at the moment, he didn't care. He hunted through the stack of ignored files until he found what he was looking for, then shoved the papers into his briefcase and snapped the case shut.

He didn't look at Dana, didn't acknowledge her in any way. She'd become a weakness in his blood, and he'd have to deal with that. *Later.* Right now, he had business to take care of.

Dana rushed alongside him as he headed for the door. "What about Ms. Markum and 'Tattle Today TV'?"

"You can tell Ms. Markum to take a flying leap—"

"R.J.!"

They were in the hallway, almost to the elevators. He gave an impatient look at his watch and wondered what Drake would have to say about being kept waiting. A first and, most definitely, a last. "Tell her whatever the hell you want, as long as it's no. I don't want a damn thing to do with that woman."

"It might be good publicity—"

He stepped into the elevator and punched the button for the lobby. "I said no, Dana. And regardless of anything else, I'm still your damn boss."

She stiffened and her soft mouth firmed into a straight line. Just before the elevator doors shut, she gave him a sharp salute and chimed, "Yes, sir!"

R.J. found himself cursing violently to an empty elevator. He hadn't meant to hurt her, but he felt totally dispossessed of every value he held near and dear. His work ethic had always been uppermost in his mind. Not once since he'd been old enough to be responsible for himself had he shirked his duties. But now, having Dana in the office had become a distraction he couldn't deal with. One look at her, and all he could think about was how wonderful her body had felt beneath his. He'd been given to daydreaming, when all his life he'd disdained the fools who wasted their time doing just that.

Marrying Dana had done as he'd hoped. With all her efforts, his reputation was in repair.

But was it a reputation he was worthy of anymore?

CHAPTER ELEVEN

DANA HURRIED IN through the garage, noticing as she parked that R.J.'s car was there, also. She had hoped to beat him home. Home. What a strange word to use in connection with a house that wasn't hers and never would be. But she did feel at ease here. And she absolutely loved the grounds. Each morning she and R.J. took their coffee to the cozy back patio. The scent of flowers combined with gurgling water from the pond fountain nearby and the chirping of birds in the yard had worked to make her feel very relaxed and peaceful. She loved it.

Of course she'd kept her apartment. For now, she could enjoy his home as her own, but she'd be going back to her place once R.J. decided the marriage had served its purpose and was no longer needed.

He'd tried to argue about that, too, she remembered, as she retrieved her packages from the trunk. He'd been so unreasonable about so many things, but to even think she'd give up her apartment and all her furnishings when the marriage wasn't the forever kind…. Never mind that he'd tried telling her he'd get her another apartment—

even a house if she wanted it—when the time came.
You'd think the man would know her better than that.

R.J. must have been listening for her, because before
she could juggle her keys to unlock the door from the
garage into the house, he was there. He still had on his
dress slacks, but he was in his socks and his hair was
disheveled. His shirt was completely unbuttoned, hanging from his broad shoulders and displaying more than
it concealed.

As usual, the sight of him did funny things to her
stomach.

"R.J.," she said by way of a greeting.

He reached out and lazily relieved her of the bags,
balancing them all in one arm. "Where've you been
to?"

His tone had a slightly edgy sound to it, and she
looked at him warily. "I went shopping."

He didn't reply, but waited until she'd stepped into the
house then closed the door behind her. He followed her
through the dining area to the kitchen. Dana pulled off
her lightweight jacket and laid it over a chair. "What's
wrong?"

"Wrong? I've been home for over an hour. The house
was empty. No wife, not even a housekeeper."

"I thought your meeting might keep you longer."

His eyes narrowed. "After lunch, I got back on
schedule." He lifted a glass from the counter and took
a healthy swallow. Ice cubes chinked as he finished it
off. "One blunder a day is enough. Besides, there was

no way I could have been late for my last meeting. As it was, half my family was there and they gave me hell for not telling them about the wedding."

Dana eyed the drink in his hand. R.J.'s sister Abby was Maitland Maternity's finest obstetrician and one of Dana's closest friends. His sister Ellie was the hospital administrator and Beth, Ellie's twin, managed the day-care center. Dana had known they would all be at the meeting, with Megan, of course. Maitland Maternity was, for the most part, a very family-oriented business. Dana had wondered how R.J. would explain away their marriage.

But at the moment the reasoning he'd given for their marriage didn't matter. She remembered that Abby had confessed her concern over R.J.'s drinking habits of late. But to Dana's knowledge, he hadn't drunk at all since the wedding.

R.J. saw the direction of her gaze and shook his head. "Don't start. Abby already gave me a earful. You'd think I'd turned into a damn lush the way she fretted."

"She loves you, so she worries."

"She has no reason. And as long as you're going to be the nosy wife, you might as well know it's only cola. I want to talk to you, and I intend to be dead sober while I do so."

That sounded far too ominous to Dana's ears. She tried for a lighthearted smile, though judging by R.J.'s frown, it wasn't effective. "Fine. Can you talk while I fix dinner?"

R.J. crossed his arms over his bare chest and scowled at her. "Why the hell are you cooking? I have a perfectly good housekeeper to do that sort of thing. Speaking of which, where the hell is Betty? She's usually here until after I get home."

Dana kept her back to R.J. as she pulled vegetables and pasta from the grocery bag then put a pot of water on the stove to boil. "I gave Betty the day off."

A beat of silence, then, "You did what?"

The low disbelief in his voice wasn't promising. Forcing a bright smile, Dana turned to head to the refrigerator. "I gave her the day off. I wanted to cook today, so I saw no reason for her to hang around."

"The reason for her to hang around is that I pay her damn well to do just that."

Dana tried to hang on to her own temper, but it wasn't easy. She'd so wanted tonight to be…special. R.J. had been so sweet all week. He touched her constantly and gave her outrageous compliments that she couldn't begin to believe but felt wonderful to hear all the same. She no longer felt so self-conscious about her looks around him. She'd even started to subtly change her appearance a bit. It wasn't much, because she'd never been the daring type, but she'd loosened her hair just a little, and had even gone so far as to let a few long strands hang free. Twice R.J. had gently smoothed them behind her ears, and she so loved having him touch her that she'd vowed to keep her hair a little less neat from now on.

And because he'd made such a fuss about her legs,

she'd taken Hope's advice and bought a pair of shoes with a slight heel. They were far from being sexy, but they didn't look like orthopedic shoes, either.

She hid a smile, remembering the attention her legs had gotten at the office all day. R.J. had even forgotten his meeting, which was an absolute first.

She waved a hand at him. "Settle down, R.J. You're a big boy. I'm sure you can get your own drink."

R.J. caught her wrist and pulled her around to face him. His expression looked as if it had been carved from flint. "I can get my own drink. But I had laundry to go to the cleaners, as well, and I like to eat when I get home, not hours later. So don't ever presume to dismiss *my* housekeeper again."

He was ruining everything with his surly temper, and Dana didn't appreciate it one bit. She jerked her wrist free and poked him in the chest. Hard. "It won't be hours if you'll get out of my way and let me cook. Pasta takes all of about twenty minutes. And if we're going to be married, even for a little while, you better learn that once I leave the office, I stop taking orders from you."

She finished that sentence with another poke, and he grabbed her hand. He looked livid, though why, she couldn't guess. She met his gaze with as much bravado as she could muster, not giving an inch. Slowly, the look in his eyes changed to one of heat, but still he didn't release her.

"You won't let me give you a damn thing, and now you want to cook, too?"

Dana rolled her eyes. "R.J., is that what this is about? I keep telling you, I don't need you to give me anything, and I enjoy cooking." She glanced down at his large hand, which was wrapped around her much smaller one. "I wanted to cook—for you."

He took a slow, shuddering breath, then released her. Turning away, he ran one hand through his hair and cursed low.

"R.J.?"

"I'm sorry," he said abruptly. "I screwed up today and I'm taking it out on you."

"Screwed up?"

He turned to face her so fast, she jumped. "I almost missed my goddamned meeting."

It was starting to sink in just how much that had upset him. Dana knew R.J. was a workaholic, that he took incredible pride in the job he did. As long as she'd been with him, he'd never missed work, and he seldom worked less than fifty-hour weeks. It wasn't that it was expected of him; R.J. demanded it of himself.

Dana pulled out a chair at the kitchen table and pushed R.J. toward it. "Sit. You can talk to me while I get your dinner ready."

He sprawled into the chair. Dana thought he looked exhausted, but he asked, "Do you want me to do anything to help?"

Just to keep his mind busy, she handed him the

package of prewashed romaine lettuce, along with a block of cheese and the shredder. "Tear the lettuce, and shred the cheese over it. Then toss on some croutons. You can put it all in this bowl."

Obediently he began tearing. As Dana began mixing up the creamy sauce for the pasta, R.J. said, "I can't be late for another meeting, Dana."

She glanced at him, worried at his tone. "I'll make sure you aren't, R.J."

"You didn't make sure today."

He wasn't casting blame so much as simply pointing out an irrefutable fact. He was in such a strange, almost dangerous mood, Dana chose her words with care. "You distracted me today. I'll be more careful from now on." He glanced up at her, and she added, "You don't have to worry about it."

He went back to shredding the lettuce. Dana didn't bother to tell him he'd already prepared enough for the two of them. She threw in the angel hair pasta, then stirred it gently.

"Actually, I do."

She kept one eye on the boiling water, one on R.J. "You do what?"

"Have to worry. I've always had to be aware of the possibility that I was more like my father than I'd like to admit."

Dana closed her eyes a brief moment as the magnitude of what he was feeling sank in. She pulled the pasta from the stove and dumped it in a colander, then rinsed it with cold water. She moved automatically, her thoughts not on preparing the meal, but on R.J. "Your father…"

"Was the blot on the family name. He left his two children without a backward glance and hasn't shown his face since." He put the lettuce aside and rubbed his forehead. "I don't want anything in common with the man, Dana, do you understand that? There'll be no comparisons. I won't forget my responsibilities."

Without really thinking about it, Dana went to the back of his chair and wrapped her arms tight around his shoulders. He lifted his hands to hold her forearms and turned his face into her. She kissed his temple. "R.J., you're the most rock steady, dependable man I've ever known."

She moved her palm to his chest and caressed him, thrilling at the feel of his warmth, of the smooth flesh over hard bone and muscle. She kissed him again, then hugged him as tight as she could.

R.J. caught her and pulled her around to his lap. His large hand turned her face up, and he said against her mouth, "I don't want you to be hurt or angry."

Confused, she whispered, "I'm not." She kissed his chin, then tucked her face against his throat. "I'm so proud of you, R.J. And I know Megan and the rest of your family are, too."

His laugh was hoarse. "They weren't proud today. They were ready to string me up for not telling them about our secret *torrid affair*."

"Oh." She leaned back to blink at him.

"They all assume we must have been carrying on behind their backs since we up and married so suddenly."

Her face flamed. "Oh, God. What must they think of me?"

"I believe Beth said something along the lines of you being a saint, since you could tolerate me and my mercurial temper. And Ellie wondered if you'd be a good influence on me."

Dana chewed her lower lip as that sank in. "Will they be disappointed when we separate?"

His thumb smoothed over her cheek. "I don't intend to disappoint anyone. That's why I made a decision today."

Dana felt awkward now that he'd gotten so serious. It looked as if it was time for that talk he'd mentioned, but she was perched on his lap and she wasn't at all oblivious to the hard evidence of his arousal beneath her. The last thing she wanted was a lecture. "Maybe we should eat first."

R.J. pulled her head to his chest, held her tight and said, "I'm firing you."

"What!"

Easily subduing her struggles, he wouldn't let her up. "Shh. You can call it quitting if you like, but the fact of the matter is, I can't have you in the office all the time. It's too distracting."

Again she struggled, and again he tightened his hold.

"Just listen, babe, okay? I did something today that I've never done before, because all I could think about was making love to you."

Dana stilled. It shouldn't matter to her, but she liked the sound of that. Maybe R.J. was starting to care for her. Maybe, just maybe, she meant more to him than a secretary or a temporary wife.

"I watched you sitting at your desk," he murmured, "and tried to imagine you there naked. You carried my papers and all I could think about was pulling you down on the carpet and opening your legs."

His words, which bordered on obscene, sounded incredibly sexy to her. Without meaning to, she knotted her hands in his loose shirt, pulling herself closer.

"I wanted you on my desk, or, hell, under my desk. Or standing up against the wall. I want you so bad, Dana. And I can't work because of it."

So she had to go. Dana hid a small smile of inconceivable joy. He wasn't manipulating her now. He had missed a meeting, and he had been distracted by her all day. Firing her wasn't just a ploy on his part to get her into his bed. He could have had her there at any point this week if he'd pushed her. But instead, he'd held back and he'd given her the most wonderful week—like a courtship.

No one would ever have accused Dana of being brazen, and now was no exception, regardless of what she was about to do. Keeping her face safely tucked against his body where he couldn't look at her, she whispered, "Then have me."

R.J. turned to stone. Dana wasn't even sure he was breathing. "Dana?"

It was a gamble, because the likelihood that R.J. would ever really care about her was remote. He'd had beautiful, sophisticated women after him his entire life, so why would he fall in love with her? But she wanted him too much to keep resisting. At least she knew his feelings, whatever they might be, were sincere. And she assumed once his frustration was taken care of, there'd be no reason for him to fire her.

She smiled and kissed his throat. "I want you, too, R.J."

He came to his feet in a rush, holding Dana close to his chest. "Right now."

Clinging to his shoulders, Dana took one quick look around the kitchen at the half-prepared meal. Reaching out, she turned off the stove, then dismissed the rest as unimportant. R.J. kept kissing her, her cheek, her hair, her ear. She almost giggled at his haste, and he squeezed her tight as he bounded up the stairs to his bedroom.

"Don't you dare laugh! Do you have any idea what I've been going through all week?" He strode down the hall, not the least winded.

Dana tangled one hand in his hair and kissed his jaw. "Since you put me through it, as well, I think I do."

"Ha. You have no idea what it's about yet. But you

will. Before the night is over, you won't have a single doubt."

He stepped into his room and kicked the door shut, then stood Dana beside the bed. She watched him, caught between nervousness and dizzy excitement as he threw back the covers on the bed and leaned toward the light on the nightstand.

Dana caught his shoulder. "R.J...." She wondered what to say as he glanced at her, then muttered, "Let's leave the lights off."

He held her gaze a moment longer, then switched on the light and straightened. "No, you don't, babe." He threw off his shirt, then sat on the side of the bed. "You're beautiful and I want to see you, all of you."

Dana felt the first sick stirrings of dread. She wasn't beautiful and—

R.J. caught her hips and pulled her between his legs. "Look at me, Dana."

It wasn't easy, but she met his determined gaze.

"I want you to trust me. Forget our first time together. I was a fool and I've been berating myself over it ever since."

Wincing, Dana slipped her hand into his hair and explained. "It's...it's not about that first time, R.J."

"I gave you no pleasure at all."

"That's not true!" It was difficult to speak because R.J. had leaned forward and was kissing her belly through the material of her skirt. She realized a second later that while he'd kissed her, he'd worked her zipper down. The skirt loosened. "R.J., I…I liked some of what you did to me that night."

R.J. reached beneath the skirt and caught the waistband of her panty hose. "Yeah. You liked it so much you refused to let me touch you again."

Her panty hose were around her ankles, and Dana, confused and off balance, stepped out of her shoes, then held onto his shoulders as he tugged the stockings the rest of the way off.

"It…it wasn't what I'd expected, R.J. That's all."

His laugh was hoarse. "I can believe that."

He reached for the buttons on her blouse and she blurted, "It was more. It was…too much."

His fingers froze on her top button, then his hands slowly lowered to her hips again. Gazing up at her with a burning intensity, he whispered, "You want to explain that?"

When she fidgeted, he pulled her onto his lap, which made it easier for her to concentrate. But the second she began to speak he started undoing buttons again. Keeping her wits together enough to measure her words was almost impossible.

She assumed that was his plan.

"Since I'd never had sex before, I thought we could… you know, do it and we'd stay detached. It would be nice but no more than that. But you touching me, kissing me, it was so…*intimate.* So personal. I felt overwhelmed and swamped with feelings and—"

His hand slipped inside her open blouse and into the cup of her bra, cuddling her naked breast. She gasped.

"Me, too, babe." His words were quietly spoken. "I felt it, too." He bent down and kissed the upper fullness of her breast, plumped up by his hand. "But part of the reason it hit me so hard was this—your beautiful body totally took me by surprise. I want to see you, Dana, and I want you to trust me enough to know I'm not lying when I tell you how sexy you are."

She didn't want to. She wanted to run away, to hide. But this was R.J., a man she'd loved since the day she'd met him and she didn't want him to be unhappy. He wanted her, and for now, that was all that mattered. "All right."

His squeeze nearly took her breath away.

Then he was lowering her to the mattress, and his hands were busy tugging away her clothes. Against her naked midriff he whispered, "This time I'll do it right, Dana. And we can both be overwhelmed."

CHAPTER TWELVE

BECAUSE she'd been so nervous, R.J. kept the light low, using only the bedside lamp. But it was enough. Soft light spilled over her nude body as she lay stretched out on his bed, highlighting the tilt of one full breast, the roundness of her thigh, the slight curve of her belly. Her skin was dewy, flushed a rosy pink all the way down to her restlessly stirring feet, and she was his.

He carefully circled one straining nipple with his tongue and heard the sexy, arousing groan Dana gave in return.

He'd been making love to her for an hour, and he wasn't at all ready to stop. He had a firm grip on his control this time, and he could easily have pleasured her, tasted her, touched her all night.

But judging by her increasingly frantic movements, the flushed heat of her skin and the silky wetness between her thighs, Dana couldn't take much more.

He hoped not. He wanted her to remember this night forever, and to know it was so special because of her, because of the incredibly feminine, sexy woman she was.

When she started to protest his lack of haste, he

sucked her nipple deep into his mouth. Her hands gripped his hair so hard he winced, then switched to the other breast.

"R.J.," she groaned, "please."

His fingers had been teasing her belly, but now he dipped them lower, gliding through her soft curls to the swollen female flesh beneath. She was hot, enticing. She was his. *Dana*. He pushed one finger into her, trying to determine exactly how ready she might be, and was surprised when she nearly climaxed, her hips jerking upward, her head arching back.

He lifted his head from her breast to look at her. "Beautiful," he breathed, and suddenly he wanted to watch her come, right now, with no more teasing.

He worked a second finger in next to the first, his mind going numb at the tightness, at the way she tensed around him, then he used his thumb to gently stroke her, finding a soft, deep rhythm. Dana strained against him, her eyes squeezed shut, her teeth clenched. Her reactions were real, with nothing held back, and he reveled in them.

"That's it, babe…"

He loved the sounds she made, without reserve or embarrassment, the sounds of a woman caught up in pleasure too intense to bear. He licked the nipple closest to him, watched her chest heave, and then she gave a low scream of pleasure.

He nearly came with her, it was such a turn-on watching *his* Dana in this way. He couldn't get over it, how innately sensual she was, yet he'd never known. She quivered, caught in the throes of her release for a long minute, before her body slowly began to go limp, relaxing against the mattress.

R.J. watched her through a nearly blinding haze of need. As soon as she'd quieted, he pulled himself over her and spread her legs wide. Again, he was struck by the realization that this was Dana, his quiet secretary, his loyal friend. His wife. It was as if her body had been made just for him. He couldn't imagine a woman any more appealing.

He lifted her knees to his shoulders, caught her buttocks in his hands and slowly pressed deep, groaning as he felt her silky, snug flesh surround him. *"Dana."*

Though she'd been utterly limp beneath him moments before, now she wrapped her hands around his upper arms and lifted her hips to meet his thrusts, giving a low moan each time.

"Am I hurting you?" he rasped, on the edge, but determined to make this as good for her as possible.

"No, no…please, don't stop."

Her breathless plea burned him. He lowered his chest to hers and kissed her, his tongue in her mouth, he was as deep inside her body as he could get.

She came with him this time, and R.J., who'd once planned to sleep alone, to maintain his privacy and his distance, locked her close to his chest as he drifted into sleep. Twice during the night she stirred, and each time he wanted her again as if the first time had never happened. She had to be tired, but not once did she complain. When she awoke to his hand stroking her breast, she reached for him and kissed him deeply.

When she rolled onto him during the night, R.J. used the moment to link their bodies and brought her fully awake by rocking into her. She bit his shoulder, then quietly succumbed to the pleasure.

Morning came too soon, but the sight of Dana sprawled in his bed, one of her slender thighs thrown over his hip, her pale hair spread out over his chest, did much to revive him. He smiled as he realized how insatiable he'd been, then smiled wider remembering how she'd reciprocated in full.

But she had to be sore, and he didn't want to be accused of being greedy, so he contented himself by stroking her awake, luxuriating in her silky skin and the fact that it was his to touch. The thought was oddly comforting.

He ran his hand down her back and over her firmly rounded behind, pushing the covers away as he did so. Dana stretched with a groan—then went abruptly still.

This was Dana's first morning after, he realized, and she looked startled, confused. As he thought about how wild she'd been through the night, he could understand why and couldn't resist teasing her a bit. "It's too late for modesty now, baby. I've already looked you over head to toe."

"R.J." She levered herself up and stared down at

him as if she were totally surprised to be in his bed. Her slumberous eyes looked deep and dark in her confusion.

Then the blush came and she quickly sat up, jerking the covers to her chin. That left him completely naked, and she indulged in some shocked staring before belatedly turning her head. R.J. stroked her hair. "It's lucky for you I have to get ready for work, or I'd remind you of how useless that blush is."

He sat up and kissed one shoulder where the sheet drooped. Dana glanced back at him, and he saw the boldness come into her eyes before she said, "If we wouldn't be late, I'd show you that no reminder is necessary."

The grin came slowly, followed by a laugh. Damn, but he liked waking up this way. He cupped the back of her head and pulled her toward him for a hard kiss. "You can sleep in, remember? As of today, you're a free woman."

He stood beside the bed and ran a hand through his sleep-rumpled hair. It was a second before he realized Dana was rigid.

In precise tones, she asked, "What are you talking about?"

Uh-oh. He took in her cold expression and the tight grip she had on the sheet at her throat and gave an inward wince. Last night, he hadn't explained completely. Not after they'd gotten sidetracked with sex.

He decided to brazen it out, and with that plan, he

sauntered to his dresser to pull out shorts and socks. Dana's gaze moved over his naked body in open fascination, but her frown didn't lessen one bit.

Another blow to his ego, he thought with wry humor.

"I told you, Dana. It's no good you working in the office with me. Do you honestly think either of us will be able to keep our minds on work?"

Her eyes narrowed. "You said that was because you wanted me. Well, you've...had me."

He chuckled at her naïveté. "And you think that's an end to it? Honey, all you've done is whet my appetite. Now that I know what I've been missing, I wouldn't get a damn thing done with you sashaying around."

She shot off the bed as if someone had lit a rocket under her. "I do *not* sashay!"

R.J. lifted one brow. "Well, I've got news for you. Whatever it is you do, it turns me on, so we're not going to find a compromise here." He went to his closet to pull out a suit. "Besides, before I came home yesterday I contacted personnel and told them to send up some applicants today. I'm going to be interviewing for a new secretary during my lunch."

There was a lethal depth to her quiet words. "You did what?"

"Megan gave me a few suggestions of employees due for a promotion. I've arranged to meet with them today."

He could feel the explosive tension emanating from

her, but he had no idea how to defuse it. He felt helpless, and that made his temper erupt. "Be reasonable, Dana. What happened yesterday can't happen again. I haven't worked this hard to be a damn good president just to throw it away because I have the hots for you. Too many people rely on me, and by God, I will not let them down."

She lifted her head like a queen and started toward the connecting door. "Fine. But you have absolutely no idea what qualities are necessary to handle your daily schedule. That's always been my job, so *I'll* pick the replacement."

"Dana…"

She whirled on him like a small tornado. "Don't you dare argue with me about this! I know the job, I'll find someone suitable for it. Period. And you can just deal with a little sexual frustration until I do." She stomped into her room and slammed the door behind her.

R.J. stood there, naked, confused, a little admiring. Dana had one hell of a temper when she let it loose. His ears were still rattling after the way she'd slammed the door. Another slow, perverse grin started. He was discovering new depths to her every day.

It made sense to let her choose her replacement; she did know the job requirements far better than he did. And now that he knew she was his at home, he could rein in his lust—*he hoped.*

Grinning, he went to the door and pulled it open and found Dana standing in the middle of the floor buck naked. She squealed and jerked a pillow from her bed to hold in front of her. "R.J.!"

Her modesty amused him, especially after how wild she'd been last night. "Hurry it along, honey. We never did eat last night, and I'm starved. We can breakfast along the way."

Her nose went into the air. "You go along without me. I have things to do this morning."

He scowled. "Like what?"

Keeping the pillow tight in front of her, she turned and headed into the bathroom, affording him a delectable view of her slender back and long legs.

"Like finding a new job, of course."

The bathroom door closed on his curse. Stubborn, obstinate, contrary—*sexy*. Why couldn't she just stay home and let him take care of her? And just who the hell did she think she was going to go to work for, anyway?

R.J. pictured another man ogling her the way he had, thinking the thoughts he'd thought, and he wanted to strangle the man without even knowing who he was.

He arrived at work that day in a bitter mood, and it only got worse as the day wore on.

MEGAN WATCHED R.J. brooding, and knew he wasn't hearing a single word she said. The moment she'd arrived, Dana had shown her into his office—an unnecessary formality, to be sure—then firmly shut the door. It wasn't often that door was kept closed, not the way R.J.

and Dana had always worked together with an almost uncanny synchronization.

Megan lowered her gaze so R.J. couldn't read the speculation there and asked, "Trouble in paradise?"

He glanced at her sharply. "What was that?"

"You're hiring a new secretary, which I'm beginning to gather wasn't Dana's idea, and she's got you closed in here like a mummy. What's going on?"

"Nothing I can't handle."

Megan looked at her oldest son fondly. "I couldn't have asked for a better firstborn than you, R.J., but sometimes you can be very shortsighted."

He fiddled with a pencil on his desk, then threw it aside. "I'm not your firstborn. I'm your first stray."

Megan stiffened. "Don't you dare insult me that way, R. J. Maitland! No, I didn't give birth to you, but by God you're mine."

Whenever she lost her temper, it always amused her children, and R.J. was no different. His mouth quirked for just a moment before he repressed the grin. "You've never shown a difference, but that doesn't mean there isn't one. If my father hadn't been so worthless and self-indulgent, you'd be my aunt, as you should be."

"True." Megan stood and paced to the window, then added, "And I remember to give thanks often for the fact you were brought to me. Regardless of the circumstances, R.J., you're my son now."

He, too, stood, and put his hands on her shoulders. "Yes."

He kissed her cheek, but Megan knew he was still buried deep in the guilt of his father, in the knowledge that he'd been "taken in." R.J. had been born with an unusual amount of pride and self-determination. Nothing she could do or say would ever diminish it until he realized that he was fully his own man, with only the parts of his father that he chose to accept.

Megan turned to him, all business now. "I'd like you to call Dana in."

"Why?" He looked disgruntled at the thought of seeing her, but he was already headed to his intercom. "Dana, if you could join us, please?"

Her voice was cool when she replied, "Yes, sir, I'll be right there."

R.J. ground his teeth.

Shaking her head at the foolishness of young love, Megan waited for Dana. She came into the room within ten seconds, but she didn't look at R.J. She merely waited.

Two such proud, stubborn people. Megan wondered when R.J. would finally realize that Dana loved him. And when Dana would finally tell him. She saw a long, bumpy road ahead of them, but she'd made it a practice not to interfere in her children's lives.

"We've had two more women check out of the clinic."

R.J. cursed. Dana rubbed her brow.

"Dana, you've done an excellent job of showcasing R.J.'s more redeemable qualities, but the matter of the baby still exists. Until we find the father or mother, the clinic is going to be under suspicion. I'm not overly worried about that, but I've decided to call Jake home."

R.J. turned to her sharply. "Do you know how to reach him?"

"He always leaves me a contact number in case of an emergency." She tried to say it with more confidence than she felt. She had no idea what her younger son was involved in. They all teased him about being a spy, but sometimes Megan wondered if there was some truth to the taunt. "Since your marriage, much of the fire has been aimed at him. He has a right to be here to defend himself, and of course, though I wouldn't say it to anyone else, there is the possibility that he's the father."

Dana glanced at R.J. "Miss Markum asked to do an interview with R.J., but he refused. I think that's why she's turned up the heat again."

Megan drew a breath. "Well, you just go on refusing, R.J. That woman will only get what we choose to give her, and she'll learn the Maitlands can't be bullied."

R.J. put his arm around his mother and said, "Be sure to let me know how Jake feels about being accused of fathering a baby by fifty different women."

"You can ask him yourself," she said with a smile. "If I have my way, he'll be here for Thanksgiving. It'll be nice to have the whole family together and it'll give Connor the chance to meet Jake."

R.J. stiffened, as Megan had known he would. But she couldn't explain about Connor, not yet.

"Have you had him investigated, Mother?"

"Soon," was all she'd say on the matter. "Now, I need to get going. I'm meeting Connor for lunch."

R.J. was still frowning after his mother was gone, the door closed behind her.

Dana glanced at him, trying to keep her expression cool. "As long as I'm here and interrupting your day, could you spare the time to give me a recommendation?"

A shock of angry disbelief darkened his eyes. "A what?"

"A recommendation. I could use it for finding a new position. I spent the morning hunting up prospects—in between interviewing your applicants, who, by the way, all failed miserably—and I have a few possibilities that seem interesting."

He advanced until he was very near her. "Let's go over this a little more slowly, if you please. What the hell do you mean my applicants all failed?"

Dana shook her head with pity. "They were all anxious for the job, no doubt about that. But they didn't have the necessary skills. What they had was a healthy hunger to bag the boss. And if you think I'm distracting, you wouldn't have lasted a minute with any of them."

"Meaning?"

"Meaning they were all young and very attractive," she said with terse disdain, then started to turn away.

R.J. caught her to him, holding her against his chest.

His gaze was probing, then his hazel eyes lightened, and though he didn't quite smile, Dana could see he was amused. "You're jealous."

Outrage bubbled up inside her because he was right. She'd taken one look at the women and dismissed them all, despite their qualifications. "Ha!" was all she could think to say.

R.J. pinched her chin and spoke in a husky whisper. "There's no need, you know. I've got a hunger for a prickly, uptight, recently debauched virgin, and no one else will do."

Her face flamed at his description, but she thought with spite that he hadn't seen the women or he wouldn't be so positive about that. She pulled her chin free. "Well, your hunger will be safe soon enough, if you'll give me the recommendation. I have two positions to look at after work, and while you were in the conference with your mother, Mr. Brashear from the supplies office down the street stopped in. He heard I'd soon be free, and he offered me a job. With a raise."

R.J. took two steps back. "No."

Quirking her brow, Dana said, "I wasn't aware it was your decision to make."

"I know Brashear. You're not working for him."

Brashear had stopped by, but Dana had dismissed him as a possibility. The position was a good one, with excellent pay and benefits, but the man was a reprobate. "Stop grinding your teeth, R.J. I'll work for whomever I please."

"Not as my wife, you won't. Hell, the man's a lecher. If he offered you a job, it's just so he can chase you around his desk!"

Dana went on tiptoe, which wasn't easy in her new shoes, and spoke straight into R.J.'s face. She was beyond furious, and the anger felt good, much better than the jealousy. "Maybe," she nearly shouted, "unlike you, Brashear recognizes my qualities as a first-class executive assistant! Did you think of that possibility?"

"No, and neither did he!"

Dana grabbed her head. "My God, you're a pigheaded man!" She stomped out of his office and into her own, this time refraining from slamming the door. It closed with a quiet click. She was in the office, after all, and as she'd just told him, she was the best executive secretary there was.

And she'd go on being that until R.J. actually forced her to leave. Not that he needed to know that.

She checked his schedule, then waited ten minutes before reminding him he had a few calls to make. She kept her tone polite—barely, and R.J. merely grunted a reply. When she inquired as to whether or not he'd written the recommendation, he slammed his finger down on the intercom button and disconnected her.

Dana grinned.

Poor R.J. He had his hands full right now, but she had to admit she enjoyed his display of jealousy. If she chose to see it as a promising sign, it was nobody's business but her own. She did feel horrible that all this was happening at such a bad time for him. His reputation was no longer being shredded, but apparently the clinic's reputation was still threatened, and she knew he was worried about Megan.

The sudden appearance of Connor was suspect, as far as she was concerned. Why would the man show up after all this time? And didn't he have any more pride than to allow Megan to pay his way?

Dana shook her head. She supposed they'd find some answers in the next few weeks. Maybe then R.J. would be able to put at least that worry to rest. After all, if Connor was telling the truth, if he was Megan's nephew, then he had a rightful place in her affections.

The door between their offices opened and R.J. stood there leaning against the frame, looking at her. Dana glanced up with a silent question.

"I'm sorry."

She was so surprised, she blinked. "What was that?"

He gave a hearty sigh and shook his head. "You want your pound of flesh, huh? Very well, I said I'm sorry."

Dana came slowly to her feet. "For what—exactly?"

"For wanting to fire you. Hell, it won't matter if I can see you or not, I'm still going to want you. And I'm still going to spend far too much time thinking about you."

She gave him a steady look. "And you don't want me working for Brashear."

He gave a brief nod.

Dana smiled, then moved closer to him. "There's a solution, you know?"

"I'm ready to hear it."

She slid one hand down his tie, then slipped her fingers between the buttons of his shirt until she felt the hot silk of his skin. She felt incredibly bold. "We could spend all our time away from the office in bed, so that you'd get your fill. Maybe then you wouldn't have the energy to think about sex here in the office."

His look was so hot she felt scorched, but he kept his expression bland enough. "That's a very workable plan. I can see you truly are experienced in managing my office dilemmas."

She chuckled, but then gasped when he picked her up and carried her into his office, shoving the door shut with his foot. He set her on her feet then turned the lock.

"There's also another idea I thought we might try." His hand went under her skirt and lifted it even as he backed her into the door, wedging her legs apart with his knee. "It's called a nooner, and I think it'd go a long way to relieving my tension so I can quit slacking off and actually get some work done."

Dana, already feeling the effects of his seeking, stroking hand, said breathlessly, "I believe I could pencil that into your schedule." Then R.J. was kissing her and she didn't say anything else.

TWENTY MINUTES LATER, R.J. was whistling as he tucked his shirt in and watched Dana struggle with her hair. Her panty hose were ruined, lying in a heap on the floor. R.J. picked them up. "I'll personally see that you have a supply kept on hand."

She sent a teasing frown his way, still trying to catch her breath. "That won't do me much good right now."

His voice dropped, and he touched her cheek tenderly. "Shall I run down to the gift shop for you?"

"No!"

He laughed. "You know, another thing we'll need to keep on hand is condoms. I'm not in the habit of carrying more than one—and that has always been for emergencies."

Jealousy flared again, though he'd just finished loving her very thoroughly. Her eyes narrowed. "Emergencies?"

"Hmm. With you tempting me all day, I expect to have a lot of emergencies."

Dana considered that, then mentioned something that she hadn't thought of before. She straightened R.J.'s tie, just so she wouldn't have to look right at him as she said it. "You didn't use protection last night."

He drew a deep breath and caught her hands. "No, and I'm sorry about that. No excuse except that you do affect me in uncommon ways. But, honey, if there's any…problem, let me know right away."

"Problem?"

"I have no interest in being a father, Dana. Now or ever. I've told you that before."

She remembered him saying as much when Tanya had claimed to be the abandoned baby's mother. But that had been Tanya.

And what made her think she was special? Dana wondered.

Every wonderful thing she'd just been feeling seemed to dissipate like mist. "I want children someday."

There was no hesitation in his answer. "That's fine. And I wish you luck." His expression hardened and he added, "Just don't expect me to be the father."

She started to turn away, wanting only to be alone, to nurse her sudden overwhelming grief without fear of him seeing too much, but R.J. caught her arm.

"If you find out you're pregnant, you'll tell me immediately. I don't think there's much to worry about, since it was only the one night, but just in case—"

"I understand." And she did. Only too well.

As Dana sat at her desk, seeing nothing but the destruction of her own silly dreams, she wondered about the little baby Megan was taking care of. What if R.J. had been the father? She could understand now why it would have made him so angry. But that poor baby.

And if it wasn't R.J., who *was* the father?

CONNOR O'HARA walked outside his Montana ranch house, ambling around the empty, expansive grounds. The November wind whistled and howled over the trees in a mournful wail, reminding him he was alone. The cold sliced through his shearling coat like thin icy blades. This wasn't Texas, he thought with a shudder, where even now the temperatures would be mild.

He looked out at the brittle, winter landscape, but he wasn't really seeing it. In his hand, the letter from the lawyer fluttered.

It was from Harland Maitland, his deceased grandfather.

His hand knotted into a fist against his thigh, crumpling the paper. He stopped to rest his back against a bare tree. So much had changed in his life. First his mother had confessed that he was adopted—a truth guaranteed to rattle anyone's foundation. But he could accept that. His mother had always been there for him, and he'd loved her dearly. Finding out she hadn't given birth to him wouldn't change that.

She'd known she was dying or perhaps he'd never have found out the truth. He'd wondered at the time who his real mother could be, but not once had he suspected the truth.

His grief and confusion had driven him to Lacy Clark, his young housekeeper. What a mistake that had been, he thought with the niggling remains of anger. She'd been so sweet, so ready to please him. And she'd seemed so wholesome, a child of nature with her long blond hair, her big innocent blue eyes. But after one night in his bed, she'd run off with someone else, or so Janelle, his mother's new maid, had claimed. He'd come home from a brief business trip to find Lacy gone. If Janelle hadn't still been there, he'd never have known what had happened to Lacy. Her betrayal had been the killing blow.

There'd been nothing left for him in Texas, so he'd dismissed Janelle, uprooted himself and moved to Montana.

But now, the lawyer's letter claimed he had a very valid reason to visit Texas again. Connor stared at the scrap of paper, more tattered than not, thanks to his bruising hold on it. That single piece of paper had affected a lot of people. He wasn't the only one involved.

The letter explained how Megan Kelly's father told a young Megan her baby had died when he'd really sold it to Harland Maitland for his daughter, Clarise—Connor's adoptive mother.

According to the letter, Megan, who'd become a Maitland after her marriage to Harland's son, William, was his birth mother. She'd thought he was dead; he hadn't known she existed.

Now the big question was, what would he do with the information?

Should he look her up and explain? Or should he leave things as they stood? After all, if Clarise had known the truth, maybe there was a damn good reason she hadn't shared it with him.

Connor turned and headed for the house. Usually the quiet of his land gave him some measure of peace, but tonight there would be no rest for him.

CHAPTER THIRTEEN

DANA WAS too quiet, and he didn't like it. R.J. watched her as they stepped into his mother's home, trying to decide what the problem could be, but she was giving away no clues. She seemed fragile, and that brought out his protective instincts like never before.

He should have been well pleased with things, R.J. thought. Dana hadn't missed her period, as he'd first feared, and his relief had been monumental. She was still working for him, but true to her word, she scheduled private, very naughty meetings for the two of them whenever possible—and Dana was a whiz with his schedule. But it didn't stop there. Now that he'd gotten her over her skewed perception of herself, she was open, sometimes even extravagant in her desire, and she matched him perfectly.

He liked coming home to her. She insisted on cooking often, and though he'd always considered Betty an excellent cook, it was different when Dana was puttering around in his kitchen. He liked to sit at the table and help, or just talk to her. Or watch the graceful, feminine way she moved. He could easily imagine doing just that for the rest of his life.

They were mobbed as they stepped in the door of his mother's home, warm and filled with the scents of roasting meats, baking bread and sweet desserts. He glanced around the room and saw his twin sisters, Beth and Ellie, immediately heading for them. Beth's fiancé, Brandon, was in close conversation with Ellie's fiancé, Sloan Cassidy. R.J. thought to join the men, but his sisters pulled him aside, hugging him and chiding him for being late. Dana laughed as she was drawn in a different direction, welcomed by his family and their friends.

"I had a few last-minute things to take care of," R.J. explained to his sisters. "Is Connor here?" R.J. had met Connor earlier, but he hadn't had the opportunity to spend much time with him.

Ellie gave him a somber look. "He's in the living room with Abby and Kyle. Come on, we'll go together."

R.J. exchanged robust greetings with his various family members as he followed Ellie. His sister Anna was already ensconced with Dana in the corner, along with Hope Logan. The women made an austere group, not one of them smiling. R.J. naturally sought out Drake, and found him propped against the buffet, scowling at his wife from across the room. R.J. pulled up short.

"Just a minute, Ellie. I want to speak to Drake first."

"Good luck." Ellie gave Drake a pitying glance. "Mother had to practically twist his arm to get him to come this year. And he's done nothing more than brood since he arrived."

R.J. frowned. That wasn't like Drake. He and Hope always joined in the family get-togethers. Hope was close friends with his sisters, and Drake, as the clinic's VP of finance, knew the entire family well.

"Drake." R.J. clapped him on the shoulder by way of greeting and got a glare in return.

"You made me spill my drink."

Laughing, R.J. took the drink from him and set it on the credenza. "If you don't get rid of your black cloud, it's going to start raining in here and ruin my mother's rug."

Drake muttered an oath, then leaned his head against the wall, his eyes closed. "I shouldn't have come."

"Nonsense. We consider you one of the family."

Drake's eyes opened, and his gaze zeroed in on his wife. "It's getting harder and harder to pretend."

R.J. watched him with a frown. "Sorry, you lost me there."

Drake's expression grew even more sullen. "Hope and I are separated."

If R.J. had been drinking, he'd have choked. As it was, he nearly choked anyway. "When did this happen?"

With a vague motion of his hand, Drake said, "It's been a while. I haven't bothered to go shouting it to the world, but I have a feeling my wife has been more than willing to."

R.J. followed his gaze to the cloister of women in the far corner and saw they were all frowning in sympathy. Yep, they were commiserating. Then he noticed that Dana looked even more upset than the others, and wondered if she, too, had personal woes she intended to reveal to the female masses. The thought didn't please him at all.

But she met his gaze briefly and offered him a tentative, sad smile.

R.J., not understanding that look, turned back to Drake. "Is it something the two of you can work out?"

"Hell, no." Drake grabbed his drink and swallowed the rest of it in one gulp. Eyes glinting, he muttered, "She wants to have kids."

"Ah." R.J. shoved his hands into his pockets and rocked on his heels. "That's a tough one."

"Hope knew how I felt about it before she married me," he said, staring at nothing in particular. "I've always been honest with her."

"But?" R.J. could sense he had more to say, and he felt totally inadequate to help Drake figure this one out. Drake's parents were as wealthy as his own, but unlike Megan and William, they'd been cold and disinterested in their children. R.J. understood how Drake felt about having children, because he felt the same. Sometimes blood rang true, and you just didn't know if you'd be good at something, like parenting, or if you'd follow in your father's footsteps. Better not to put it to the test.

At the same time, he truly hated to see Drake in such torment. It had always been blindingly clear how much he and Hope loved each other. They were meant to be together.

Drake poured another drink. "But...nothing."

R.J. cleared his throat. He remembered when his nephew Will was born, the instant surge of love and protectiveness he'd felt, the overwhelming emotions. "One thing about kids, they can sure as hell throw you for a loop."

Drake gave him a bleak look. "I don't know much about kids, R.J. And what I do know is sure as hell not worth remembering."

R.J. lifted one brow, then again looked at Dana. She'd been speaking very quietly with Hope, but as if she'd felt his gaze, she looked up. Her smile was gentle, her green eyes soft. He saw the emeralds at her wrist and throat and his ring on her finger. "I haven't a clue how to help you, Drake. I just hope you and Hope can work this out."

Just then Megan called for everyone's attention. R.J. turned and felt his sister Anna slip up beside him, hooking her arm through his. Will, her son, who at ten liked to think himself very worldly, leaned against R.J.'s side. Because he'd done it so many times, R.J. ruffled his hair, then rested his hand on Will's head.

Everyone gave their attention to Megan.

"I'm sorry to tell you, but Jake phoned to say he won't be able to make it, after all. He'll be home by Christmas, but for today, we'll just have to get by without him."

Anna gave R.J.'s arm a squeeze. "I wish I knew exactly what it was Jake did for a living."

R.J. glanced at her, then shrugged. "Something with

the C.I.A. or the F.B.I., no doubt. Or maybe he's really a street cleaner and just doesn't want us to know. That's why he pretends it's so hush-hush."

Anna laughed as R.J. hunkered down next to Will. "What about you, kiddo? You want to be a spy someday?"

Will pretended to think about that, his young face drawn in lines of concentration. "Nah. Mom needs me to stick around. She'd be lonely if I left."

R.J. gave him an approving hug. "That's the attitude!"

Will rushed off when the doorbell rang again, and R.J. watched him go with a smile. Anna smacked his arm. "You've got him acting as overprotective as you do."

R.J. sniffed in mock hauteur. "Grant the men in your life a little right to worry, all right?"

"Little would be the operative word there. You tend to hover in excessive amounts."

R.J. knew she was teasing. "Anna, can I ask you something?"

"Uh-oh, sounds serious. And here I thought you'd still be floating on a cloud of marital bliss."

"Actually, I am. Floating that is. Dana is…" He floundered, looking for the right words. Dana meant so much to him, and always had. He'd just never realized it before. He hated to admit it, but he'd taken her for granted when she was the most important person in his life.

"She's Dana. And you know she's loved you forever. Though I may never forgive you for not having a big wedding, I'm willing to cut you some slack for finally wising up and loving her back."

R.J. gave her such a blank look, Anna groaned. "Don't tell me you didn't know?"

He shook his head, then once more sought out Dana with his eyes. His heart was racing. He'd been so blind, so stupid. He'd almost ruined things between them. "You think she loves me?"

"Don't be a dope, R.J. Why else would she have married you?"

Why else, indeed? He thought of how she'd always doted on him, how well she knew him and what he wanted or needed and when. The way she seemed attuned to his every thought. She was more than he'd ever imagined possible in a woman, and certainly more than he deserved. He continued to watch her. "I never thought I'd make very good husband or father material."

Anna put her hand to his cheek, gaining his attention. "I'll admit you're overbearing, and your temper is too quick, and you're autocratic—"

"Enough, brat!"

"But you're also one of the finest men I've ever met. I can't imagine any man being a better father or husband than you. Will adores you. Just look at how you've always been with him."

Just the word *father* made R.J. feel a little sick inside.

He said, a touch of desperation in his tone, "I'm Will's uncle, there's a big difference."

"Not when there is no father. If it hadn't been for you, Will would have missed out on so much."

R.J. pulled her into a tight embrace and rocked her. He loved his little sister fiercely and would have challenged the world for her. "It's not your fault the marriage didn't work."

Against his suit coat, she mumbled, "But his own father took off, and *you* filled in. Not just as an uncle, R.J., though that's responsibility enough. But you have been a father to him, too. A wonderful father. And a friend and an excellent role model. How you've been with Will, the easy, comfortable way you've always handled him, says a hell of a lot about the type of father you'd be."

R.J. felt a loosening in his chest, a tiny crack in the stone wall of his resistance. He couldn't remember a single moment he'd spent with Will that hadn't been enjoyable. From the diaper stage to the teething stage to the repeating-every-curse-word-he-said stage, Will had been a joy. Because he'd been so aware of his possible shortcomings, R.J. had worked extra hard to make certain he offered the best influence possible. He hadn't wanted to screw up with Will.

Could Anna be right? Could he handle being a father?

He tried to imagine how he'd feel with a son or daughter of his own, and a lump the size of a grapefruit filled his throat. The idea scared him spitless, but it also brought about the image of Dana as the mother, and she fit that role so beautifully, he wanted to go to her then, to tell her, to admit…that he loved her.

He closed his eyes as the reality of it sank in. God, he loved her. She'd turned his world upside down and made him see things about himself he'd never suspected. Good things. And she did it all while asking for nothing in return except physical love.

Because she assumed she'd never have any other kind from him.

"You're crushing me, R.J."

With a muttered apology, he released Anna, then ignored the way she laughed at him. He wanted to pick up his wife and carry her out of there. He wanted to be alone with her, to tell her that despite his remaining doubts, he'd be willing to try fatherhood—for her. *With her.* Hell, he'd try anything to keep Dana happy.

But before he could make that decision, a man approached, and he knew without an introduction that it was none other than Connor.

R.J. eyed him closely. He looked to be around forty, with calculating bright blue eyes and dark hair. R.J. mistrusted him on sight, though he said nothing because of Megan.

His mother hovered nearby, and R.J. stuck out his hand, not wanting Megan to sense his reservation. After all, he'd once been a stray himself. "Connor. Good to see you again. Sorry it's been a while."

The man nodded, and his grip was a little too tight to be called polite. "I just figured you didn't have any time to spend with your new cousin."

There was blatant challenge in his words and grip, and R.J.'s instincts went on alert. In the next instant Dana was there at his side. She always seemed to know when her calming influence was needed.

Dana was cool, poised, and she could defuse a situation with her mere presence. While Dana made social chit-chat with Connor, R.J. focused on his love for his wife rather than his distrust of this long-lost cousin. He felt full to bursting, and not even a hostile confrontation could dent his newfound inner peace.

Megan announced that dinner was ready. R.J., his arm around his wife, put his worries from his mind and enjoyed his family and friends and his newly realized love. The evening progressed smoothly. He watched Drake and Hope, and wished for some way to help them. Megan brought the baby down, and somehow R.J. ended up with the little scamp in his lap. Though his hands trembled and his heart raced, it wasn't a horrible feeling. He thought of how close he'd come to being named the baby's father, and suddenly, it didn't seem like such a horror. Holding the infant, he could understand Megan's feelings, how she'd immediately begun loving him.

Deliberately, R.J. carried the baby across the room, bypassing all the women with their outstretched arms, to place the little boy in Drake's lap, instead. Hope immediately settled beside him, her eyes soft with maternal yearning, while Drake went stiff as a poker.

R.J. laughed, surprising everyone. Love could work miracles; Drake didn't stand a chance.

He caught Dana's hand and announced to his family and friends that he was calling it an evening. Since the night was still young, he accepted the ribald comments tossed out about newly married couples.

He and Dana were silent on the ride home, but R.J. was content. He parked the car and opened her door for her, then followed her inside. They climbed the stairs together, and already R.J. was hard with wanting her. The feeling was different now that he knew he loved her, that he'd make this marriage the forever kind, just as Dana deserved.

They stepped into her bedroom and he caught her shoulders, turning her to face him.

Before he could orate on his love, however, she beat him to the punch. She stared at him, her beautiful eyes solemn, and said, "I can't do this anymore, R.J. I'm moving back to my own place."

FOR A SINGLE HEARTBEAT, R.J. turned to stone. It felt as if the blood had frozen in his veins. Then determination set in. He'd be damned if he'd let her walk away after he'd just come to such a life-altering revelation.

Nodding slowly, his hands clasped behind his back in a pose that he hoped would hide his anger, he asked, "Care to tell me why?"

She paced over to the window, looking out on the grounds she'd always admired so much. "I love you, R.J."

"Ah." He thought he might explode with happiness. He felt taller, stronger. "Obviously a good reason to leave a man."

She toyed with the edge of the curtain, uncertainty obvious in the tilt of her head. "You don't understand…."

"You've never accused me of being a stupid man before, sweetheart. Let's not start now, okay?" That fragile look settled over her again. He wanted to hold her and decided there was no reason not to.

She looked startled when he strode across the room and scooped her up. "R.J.!"

"Shh. You're my wife." He laid her across the bed and sat beside her. The dress she'd worn was more feminine than her usual attire, and he'd remarked to her earlier how anxious he was to get her out of it. That urgency hadn't abated one bit, but first he had to take care of other things. "Did you know Drake and Hope are separated?"

Dana turned her head away, but quickly faced him again. His wife was no faint heart. "Yes. I've known for some time. Hope wants children. I…I thought about that, R.J. She's hurting so much, and I can't help but put myself in her shoes. Every day…" She swallowed hard, then continued. "Every day I love you more. I thought I could do this, thought I could play house, and wife, and enjoy the time I had with you, but every time we have sex—"

"Make love."

She paused, then nodded. "Every time it makes it so much harder to think of leaving. But you've made it plain you don't want this forever. You don't want kids, and—"

"I've changed my mind." He wanted to laugh at the way her eyes widened and her mouth fell open. Instead, he bent down and kissed her gently. "I have no idea what kind of father I'll make, Dana, yet Anna assures me I'll handle it just fine." His forehead touched hers, and he sighed. "I'm not my father, I know that, but as his son I was afraid I might carry a legacy of paternal disinterest."

"Oh, R.J." She looked equal parts amazed, sympathetic and annoyed. "For an intelligent man, that's not a very sound deduction."

He didn't take offense; he agreed with her. "I know. But I couldn't bear the thought of doing what he'd done, abandoning a child of my own, feeling no emotional tie or responsibility...."

"It's called love," she explained gently, "and you've already proven—to everyone but yourself, I guess—that when you love, you don't hold back. Anna knows that, as do Will and Megan and all the rest of your family." Her hand smoothed over his nape, and her smile was gentle. "You're an absolutely wonderful man, and I know you'd make a wonderful father."

R.J. accepted her words, then added, "But only with you. If you leave me now, Dana, well, then, I guess I'll just remain the most eligible bachelor in Austin, because I sure as hell won't settle for anyone other than you. Not after seeing how perfect you're suited to me."

She looked like a statue, staring at him, not moving, not even blinking. R.J. turned and pulled off her shoes, tossing them over his shoulder to the floor. He felt exuberant and excited. He was painfully aroused. "I think I may be ready to give fatherhood a try. The idea of you carrying my baby turns me on." He grinned at her. "But if you have any doubts…"

"No."

She sat up to regain his attention, and R.J. reached behind her to the fastenings of her dress. "Good. Your faith in me never ceases to boggle my mind."

"R.J.—"

The dress slipped over her shoulders, leaving her in her strapless bra. R.J. whistled. "Damn, honey, when did you get that?"

Distracted, she explained, "Hope and Anna bought me some things."

He fingered the lace edging the cups of the bra. "More things like this?"

"Yes. R.J., stop that." She pushed his hands away, then pressed on his shoulders. R.J. pushed back, and gently tumbled her onto the bed. "R.J.…."

He kissed her ribs as he tugged the dress down. "Another thing, honey." The dress bunched at her hips, and

R.J. lifted his head to look at her. Tears were in her eyes, ripping his heart out. "I love you."

She gasped, and the tears spilled over. "You love me?"

He settled at her side, then gathered her against his chest. "So much, Dana. Damn, I've been stupid." She stirred, and he squeezed her tight to keep her in place. "No, don't defend me."

"I was going to agree!"

He laughed. Much as Dana loved to defend him, she didn't pull any punches, either. She was, as he'd told her, perfect for him. "Good. Because I've been a blind fool. My only excuse is that you let me be blind. I'll trust in the future that you'll keep me better informed of things I should know."

Dana wriggled out of his hold to prop her elbows on his chest. The position did delightful things to her breasts and made the urgency beat at him. The emerald necklace hung free, the light glinting off it. "Tell me again," she said.

"That I love you? I do. And I need you. And I want you."

She pressed her hips down. "The want part I can believe. You've got proof."

He stilled her hips by gripping them in his large hands. "The love and need part you can believe, too. I don't want you to have any doubts, Dana. Not about me and what I feel for you. I've known so many women over the years, but none of them affected me like you do. I've been obsessed with you, but I didn't even know why."

"You've been obsessed with sex." She kissed him. "Not that I'm complaining."

R.J. pulled her back for a more thorough tasting that left them both breathless. "This isn't mere sex, woman. Sex I could have with any number of women. What we have together is special, and if you don't tell me you'll stay with me and love me and have my babies, I'll…"

"Fire me again?"

"Smart ass."

"Smart enough to know a good thing when I have it. I'm not going anywhere, R.J." She laid her head on his chest. "All I ever wanted was for you to love me."

"I seem to recall you demanding sex rather forcefully, too."

"R.J.!"

His grin was wicked. "As a businessman, I have to say that was the best deal of my life."

Dana met his grin with one of her own. "Then I think you should stop talking and start fulfilling your end of the bargain."

R.J. agreed. After all, regardless of his father's tainted legacy, he was no slacker. And he'd proved it.

* * * * *